Bait N' WITCH

BRIMSTONE  INC.

Bait N' WITCH

BRIMSTONE ✪ INC.

ABIGAIL OWEN

Entangled Publishing, LLC
10940 S Parker Rd
Suite 327
Parker, CO 80134
rights@entangledpublishing.com

Amara is an imprint of Entangled Publishing, LLC.

Edited by Heather Howland
Cover design by Bree Archer
Cover photography by KDdesignphoto and f11photo/Shutterstock

Manufactured in the United States of America

First Edition June 2020

*To my children, who bring magic
into my life every single day.*

Chapter One

Rowan pulled her borrowed truck up the gravel drive and parked in front of a rustic mountain cabin.

She frowned. This couldn't be right, could it?

It took a second to realize she'd lifted her foot off the brake, the truck rolling forward like it, too, wanted to escape from here.

She put it in park and again checked the directions she'd been provided. It'd been a long time since she'd had to follow directions to travel anywhere. Too bad she couldn't use her teleporting skills like usual. But witches who had to get jobs as nannies weren't supposed to possess that kind of power. If she was going to pull this off, she had to pretend she had minimal magical abilities and not show her true capabilities.

The paper in her hand matched the address on the quaint mailbox. Damn. She *was* at the right place.

"Fantastic," she muttered.

The two-story cabin—a lovely and obviously old log structure built into the gentle bottom slope of a mountain— was tucked away in the wilderness of the Rocky Mountains in Colorado, among copses of aspens and pines. Not another dwelling for miles, which meant she was well and truly screwed if this plan went sideways.

The back of Rowan's neck prickled like there was a spider crawling along her skin. She went to brush it away, then stopped herself mid-swipe and jerked her hand back with an irritated huff. That prickly feeling had been her constant companion for the last year. The one that said she was being watched, even when she knew she wasn't. Ever since she'd been taken by that werewolf. Only she wasn't with him anymore, nor with the people who'd helped him. He was dead, and his people were, too.

No. This had to be more about the man inside the house…

"Suck it up and get moving," she instructed herself.

How had circumstance brought her to this point? The fates must really have it in for her.

Tally up the sum total of what brought her to this moment: Parents killed in a mysterious accident. Her adopted mother, Tanya, a demon masquerading as a witch, being murdered by Kaios, a pathologically insane werewolf. Kaios who had then taken Rowan prisoner for her unique powers and used her against her will for his own ends.

At least that asshat was dead now.

Still…too many dings against her. The Covens Syndicate— the body of witches and warlocks who monitored, policed, protected, and ruled the established covens throughout the world—were sure to issue a death sentence once they finally found her. Hell, the other warlock Kaios had forced to do his bidding had been executed summarily without trial, and he'd only had the "controlled by a werewolf" thing against him.

The Syndicate tended to execute first, ask questions later.

When it came to Rowan's parents' deaths, Tanya had always wondered who was to blame…

Stick to the plan.

The immensely dangerous, undeniably brilliant plan, courtesy of Delilah at Brimstone, Inc. The woman had rescued her, hidden her, and now sent Rowan off to save her own life. Assuming this worked.

Delilah.

No last name. Not a witch. In fact, Rowan wasn't sure what Delilah was, though something about her felt…familiar. Regardless, she was obviously powerful. The woman practically crackled from within when she walked into a room. Tons of connections with all things paranormal.

Even with that, when Rowan added it all up, she had basically hopped from one bad situation to another.

And now, here I am, about to pose as a nanny for the witch hunter the Syndicate set on me.

That was Delilah's plan—hide Rowan in plain sight, right under the hunter's nose, close enough to cause problems with the investigation, making it impossible for the Covens Syndicate to track her down.

Now that she was here, she was starting to have an eleventh round of second thoughts.

With a trepidation worthy of Daniel when he entered the lions' den, she got out of her truck and approached the perfectly normal-looking front door. Of course, by entering this household, the lions' den was exactly where she'd be. She literally faced the jaws of death, which could snap shut at any second.

Where's my whip when I need it?

She raised a shaking hand to the door and glared at the offending appendage, annoyed at her inability to control the tremor. A shrill scream pierced the air, and Rowan froze mid-knock.

"What in the name of the mother?" Instinct had her reaching for the doorknob.

Locked.

A quick incantation sprang to her lips, but, before she could utter it, the door unlocked on its own and swung smoothly open. Rowan didn't question, but instead rushed inside. Following the sound of a struggle, including several more screams, she hurried down a long hallway off the foyer to what appeared to be the family room.

The scene she came upon had her hesitating in the doorway. Three identical girls, around the age of twelve or thirteen, flung spells at each other in rapid succession and with angry intent behind every blow. In their midst stood a tall man, so handsome his looks registered even as she was figuring out what to do. His lips pinched with frustration as he tried to put a stop to things.

As far as Rowan could tell, the girls were using their magic to disfigure each other. Even as she watched from the shadow of the doorway, one wailed as her hair sprouted, lengthening until it touched the ground in a waterfall of follicles.

"Hey," the girl squealed.

"Now Chloe—" the man tried in a placating voice.

But Chloe wasn't listening. "I'll show you," she shouted. With a whisper of words and a fling of her hands, one of the other girls suddenly turned bald.

Another piercing scream of fury rent the air.

"Lachlyn, don't you dare—"

Again, the man's words went unheeded and next thing, Chloe's long hair turned mint green.

The third girl laughed, and both her sisters turned on her together, faces red with anger.

"Enough!" Rowan snapped the word, voice full of authority as she stepped into the room. With a wave of her hand, all three girls abruptly sat on the pale leather couch, mouths snapped shut and hands in their laps, held mute and immobile by Rowan's spell. She would not release them until they understood the consequences of their actions.

The man whirled on her, hands raised, glowing blue orbs of energy already formed and sparking in his palms, ready to blast her. However, Rowan had expected his action and stayed still, doing nothing to provoke him further. After all, if a total stranger showed up in her home casting spells, she'd fry them and ask questions later.

If anything, she found his restraint impressive.

"Who are you?" he demanded in a low voice.

The smooth rumble of it reminded her of the first time she'd heard a timpani drum in an orchestra as a child, the sound rolling through her chest and lodging in her mind. Shock stirred along with a rush of...need. She hadn't felt need for a man in...she couldn't remember how long.

What the hell and fairy bells?

The fates truly did have it in for her. What jokester thought attraction for this particular man would be remotely funny? Because Rowan damn sure wasn't laughing.

Now that the chaos had ceased, she studied him more closely, trying to reduce the need strumming her nerves by logically categorizing the sum of his parts.

A widowed father to almost-thirteen-year-old triplets, he was also the lead witch hunter for the Covens Syndicate. She'd expected someone in his mid-forties at the youngest, picturing distinguished gray at his temples and the onset of wrinkles. Maybe even a gut. Not that every middle-aged man looked that way, but every middle-aged warlock she'd ever happened across did.

Her mental image was a far cry from the warlock standing before her. She tallied up the essentials: mid-thirties, lean, intense, jet-black hair without a trace of gray in sight, and dark eyes currently sparking with anger and magic. Like a panther lying in wait for unsuspecting prey to wander under the tree where he lurked.

A warning she took seriously, answering in a quiet, calm

voice. "Mr. Masters—"

"How do you know my name?"

"I'm your new nanny."

"Like hell you are."

Screw patience. She rolled her eyes. "Call Delilah if you don't believe me."

She had no idea how Delilah had managed to make Greyson Masters think it was his idea to have Brimstone hire his latest in a long line of nannies. She didn't ask the woman questions like that.

Still holding the crackling energy weapons in his hands, Greyson ran an assessing gaze from the tip of her untamed hair to her sneaker-clad toes and a jacket too thin for the late fall chill. Rowan did her best not to shift under his scrutiny, an unaccustomed feeling of vulnerability crawling up her spine like spiders. She wondered what he saw. Would her long red curls be the dead giveaway she feared? Would he recognize her as the witch he currently hunted? She'd considered changing the color, but that would require constant concentration to hold, or permanent hair dye that would quickly show her roots as fast as her hair grew. Besides, witches tended toward red hair more than any other color.

His face remained a mask, a total blank, giving none of his opinions away. Finally, he stood from his crouch, lowering his hands. A whispered word sent the energy balls spiraling into the air, where they expended their power in a series of tornado-like moves until they dissipated.

"Remove your spell from my children." An order, not a request.

"Certainly." As soon as she checked something first, Rowan turned to the girls. "Are you all finished?"

Three sets of wide, Caribbean-blue eyes stared at her. Correction…two sets, and a shaggy head of mint-green hair.

"I asked you to remove your spell," Greyson Masters

snapped.

She flicked him a glance. "I will. As soon as I get a guarantee of good behavior."

Rowan ignored the tightening of his mouth. Apparently, Mr. Masters was a man who expected instant obedience. And got it, too, she suspected, except from his daughters, a notion which had her lips twitching. Poor powerful warlock couldn't handle three pint-sized witches.

She turned to the girls with raised eyebrows and waited. After questioning glances at their dad, who said nothing, slowly, all three heads bobbed in agreement.

"Excellent." Rowan flapped a hand, and the girls worked their jaws and rubbed at their wrists, as though the restraints had been physical.

Command obeyed, she turned back to the father, who eyed her narrowly. Perhaps this was not the most auspicious beginning to their relationship as boss and employee. She was supposed to be lying low, avoiding scrutiny—she might have to revisit that plan.

Rowan gave a mental shrug. In for a penny, in for a pound. With a cheerful smile, she held out her hand to shake. "My name is Rowan McAuliffe." Her light brogue thickened as she spoke her name, which happened only when she was nervous.

To give him credit, Greyson at least shook her hand. "Greyson Masters."

Rowan had to keep from yanking her hand back as an almost painful electric zing shot from Greyson's hand through her body, the current sizzling down her veins, leaving in its wake heat that spread everywhere. The warmth left her unbalanced and unbelievably turned on. Until, just as quickly, the sensation drew back as though sucked in, condensing to a single smoldering spot in her left wrist.

What was that?

Carefully, she released his hand and dropped hers to her side, resisting the urge to glance at the spot, which still burned.

Those fates had some serious explaining to do. Had her traitorous body seriously lit up like the sparks that her adopted mother would give off when she was angry? All in response to that one brief touch? Pathetic. Worse, he was now her employer, and given his job to hunt her down, that reaction landed under the title of highly inappropriate. Not to mention inopportune, inexplicable, and all sorts of other words beginning with "in."

Releasing her, Greyson crossed his arms, feet planted wide. In his blue button-down and tie, the man looked more like an intimidating lawyer than a powerful mage. "How'd you get in the house?"

She blinked at the unexpected question before she remembered how the door had unlocked itself. "I was about to knock when I heard screaming." She darted a glance at the girls, who watched in rapt silence. "The door was locked, and I was about to...uh...deal with that, when it unlocked and swung open on its own."

Thick eyebrows drew down over distrustful eyes. "That's not possible. The wards on this house prevent anyone but family from coming inside without an express invitation from me or my blood relations."

"Perhaps the house sensed I was trying to help?" She wasn't quite sure what he expected her to say. She had no idea why the darn door had opened for her.

"Perhaps." Doubt dripped from two syllables. In other words, he suspected her of foul play.

Another long, uncomfortable staring session commenced, one from which she refused to back down. After being raised by a demon, intimidating stares did little to sway her. When he uncrossed his arms, she silently crowned herself the winner of this round.

"We were expecting you two days ago," he said.

"Teleporting is not one of my gifts." Total lie. Gods, she hated lying, even if she'd gotten good at it. "I got here as quickly as the speed limit allowed." Or maybe she'd taken her time. Could anyone who knew her full situation blame her?

"Hmmm…"

Rowan flashed another cheery smile and gave him her best impression of an oblivious dingbat with wide, guileless eyes. At least, she hoped that was the impression she'd leave him with.

He did not smile back. "Now that you are here, I'll go over the ground rules. We can figure things out from there."

Damn. That friendly act usually did the trick. Greyson Masters had the makings of a total scrooge. Scrooge McMasters. "Okay."

He turned to his daughters. "Let's clean you up first." Greyson raised his hands, but before he could perform the spell, Rowan cleared her throat.

He turned to glance over his shoulder at her, aggravation at the interruption clear in his gaze and pinched mouth.

"Excuse me, Mr. Masters, but shouldn't the girls clean up their own mess?"

Greyson dropped his hands, suspicion once more narrowing his eyes. "Children under the age of sixteen aren't allowed to practice magic beyond the most basic of spells outside of school unless it's with a licensed instructor. As a professional nanny for witches, I would expect you to already know that rule."

Ding. Dang. Dong. This witch was going to be dead if she kept screwing up.

The problem was, Rowan hadn't been raised by witches, and, therefore, didn't know the guidelines under which they operated. Delilah had given her a book outlining the

Syndicate's laws, which governed all the covens. Probably 90 percent or more of the covens of the world knew the rules by heart. Lived them every day.

Delilah had advised her to memorize the book or her cover would be blown. Rowan had read the thing, trying to take it all in. Only what she'd discovered was that witches raised in the covens had a shit-ton of policies to follow. How they ever got anything done was a total mystery.

Bluff, her mind screamed as she scrambled for a suitable answer.

"Of course," she said, stalling for time. "However, I am a firm believer that children should be taught to fix their own messes or live with the consequences."

"But I can't fix this," Chloe whined under her avalanche of hair.

Rowan spread her hands in an "oh well" gesture. "Maybe walking around looking like the green version of Big Foot for a while will teach you not to use magic against your sisters next time."

"We don't use magic against other people, ever, in this house. Adults included." Greyson's gaze slashed toward her, and she knew his admonishment was aimed at her as much as the girls. No wonder he needed help with the triplets if that was a rule.

"How's that working out for you?" Oh hell, hexes, and damnation. If she could've reversed time and held back that comment, she would've.

"Ms. McAullife, are you this much trouble in all your households?"

She'd never nannied before, but she couldn't tell him that. All part of her cover. "I wouldn't classify it as trouble, exactly."

"Of course you wouldn't," he muttered under his breath. More loudly, he said, "What would you classify it as?"

"Helpfulness?"

"Hmmmm…" His tone said otherwise. Conversation ended, he turned to the girls again. "This is Chloe, Lachlyn, and Atleigh." He indicated each girl with a wave.

Rowan gave them a smile, though she wasn't sure if Chloe could see her.

"The girls have school during the day. Teleportation is one of my gifts and how we travel most often. However, I will arrange for a transport key for your use on those occasions when I'm not available to take them and for weekends."

So far so good.

"It is your job to get them up and ready in the mornings. After school you will take them to an hour of magic practice with their Aunt Persephone next door to the east through the woods. She's licensed to teach them. Afterward, you'll return here, where the girls will complete any homework. They may read in the evenings."

Was he serious? No hint of teasing penetrated a rather grim expression. Yup. Serious.

Oblivious to her thoughts, he continued. "You will be in charge of all meals. Breakfast will be just you and the girls. You'll send lunch with them. And I'll join you for dinners. After dinner you'll clean up while the girls prepare for bed. They have an hour in the evenings to themselves before bed. Any questions?"

Tons. None he'd appreciate, she suspected. "Um…do the girls have any time to play or relax? What about TV? Or do they have friends they visit or who come here?"

He lifted an imperious eyebrow. "I'm not a monster. Once homework is complete, they can do what they like as long as they stay within a mile of the house. I'll let you know if friends schedule visits. Saturdays you will arrange to take them to various educational activities. Sundays, they visit their grandparents. That is your day off."

He glanced at her jeans, long-sleeved white T-shirt, and sneakers. "I expect you to dress appropriately at all times."

Glancing at his own immaculate gray pants and ironed button-down all tucked in, she surmised he meant more formal than jeans. She pictured her limited wardrobe—she'd been a prisoner for some time, and, since her release, hiding out for months, after all. She gave a mental groan. This job just got better and better.

"I'll go shopping this weekend," she murmured.

"Excellent." He flicked a glance at his watch. "I will be in my office the rest of the day. I suggest you get settled and get to know the girls."

What kind of father spent Saturday working when it sounded as though he barely saw his children during the week? "Fine."

"Any questions?"

"Which room is mine?"

Despite the extra sugar she'd imbued in the words, he still narrowed his eyes. Was her sarcasm leaking through?

"Yours is the only bedroom in the basement."

Relegated to the basement, which told her exactly where she stood in this family. Good thing ghosts didn't tend to haunt her.

He paused in turning away to cast her a final assessing look. "Dinner is at seven."

"And not a second later," she muttered under her breath. Jeez, this guy was wound tighter than a pocket watch.

He gave her a hard stare, which she returned with a guileless expression that apparently had no effect on him.

"You may call me Mr. Masters." With that, the infuriating man turned and calmly left the room.

His imperious tone decided it for her. She was going to enjoy thwarting this arrogant warlock at his own game.

Chapter Two

Rowan breathed a tiny bit easier in Greyson's absence, a reaction she put down to who he was, rather than to her odd attraction to the man. No way was she giving that any legitimacy. The spark was magical—and not in a metaphoric sense. Powerful witches and warlocks gave off a sort of electric charge. She'd cast a spell to mask hers and hopefully make him think her powers more minimal than they were. But that didn't mean she was unaffected by his aura.

Already she was regretting coming at all. What had Delilah been thinking?

Strangely, Rowan trusted Delilah. Other than Tanya, the demon who'd raised her after her parents died and had trained her in magic, no one else had come close to gaining her trust like that, which is why she'd agreed to the crazy plan.

Not for the first time, she questioned her reasoning.

Pulling her gaze from where Greyson Masters had disappeared, she glanced down and realized she was rubbing at her wrist, where he'd shocked her earlier. The spot still tingled, a warmth pulsing in tune to her heart, though the burning sensation had let up.

What on earth was that?

Raising her hand to inspect her skin more closely, she discovered a faint white line in the center of the heat. *Nuts and gnomes. I don't need anything else happening.*

"Are you really going to leave us like this?" a small voice sounded from behind her, pulling her focus away from her wrist.

Spinning around, she faced down her new charges—three miniature witches who watched her with wary curiosity. Rowan didn't see three wayward girls she had no idea how to control. Instead, three little girls who needed attention and love tugged at her heart. She knew because she'd seen that look before. Her own parents, from the little she could remember, had been equally focused on her magic more than on her as a person who needed cuddles and bedtime stories.

Things had changed with Tanya. She may have adopted Rowan, but she was the only true mother she'd ever known.

She gave the girls a gentle smile. "You got yourselves into it. You can get yourselves out."

Rowan had to hold in a laugh at the disgruntled expressions tipped toward her direction.

"I need to get my bags and unpack." At the doorway she paused and stuck her head back in the room. Two and a half sets of wide eyes, with a touch of resentment now, stared back at her. She gave her head a jerk. "Come on, then."

She left shaggy, blondie, and baldy eyeing each other on the couch and headed outside. Not much to gather—exactly one suitcase, bag and clothing both provided by Delilah. They couldn't risk going back to Rowan's place to get her stuff, not with Greyson hunting her. The Syndicate might not know who she was—yet—but that didn't make her apartment in New Orleans safe.

She rubbed at an itch on her nose, still getting used to the dry climate of Colorado, then heaved the suitcase over the side of the truck bed. Leaning to one side against the weight, she swung around, only to stop short at the sight of all three girls, appearances back to normal, watching her from the front porch.

Interesting.

"Is that all you brought?" one of the triplets asked.

"Yes." Rowan made her way up the steps, uneven and worn into smooth dips with decades worth of feet treading them over the years. She paused at the top, taking in their appearances. Greyson Masters was going to have his hands full with these three beauties. Long, honey-blonde hair, aquamarine eyes, peaches-and-cream complexions. And three of them. Rowan cocked her head as she picked up a faint mark on each of their foreheads.

"Who is who now?" she asked. She had a pretty good guess, but she wanted to be sure.

One at a time, each gave her name. The mark on each forehead was different, but she recognized them now. Variations on the runes for protection. A different one for each girl.

Placed there with kisses of protection? Why would they need such a spell? And who had placed them there?

Regardless, those came in handy. She quickly committed the symbol and name combination to memory.

She continued inside. "Maybe you should come shopping with me? You can help me choose."

Atleigh rolled her eyes. "Our last nanny wore black all the time. Are you going to do that, too?"

Not her first choice. "Is that what Mr. Masters prefers?"

"No. Daddy never said anything about how our other nannies dressed."

Probably because each had dressed like a perfect nanny. How long would it be before Greyson figured out Rowan was a total fraud?

"Which way is the basement?" Wandering the house searching did not sit well with her.

"This way." Chloe, who'd been silent up till now, led the way through the house to the kitchen and pulled open a white painted door, which could easily be mistaken for a cupboard.

Hefting her suitcase, Rowan clumped down a steep set of worn wooden stairs. To her surprise, all three girls followed. In the basement, she found a suite complete with comfy couch and TV in the living area. The far wall boasted windows and a private sliding glass door leading outside, made possible by the way the house was built into the side of the mountain. The windows let in light, creating a cozy, bright atmosphere.

Perfect.

Off the living area, which she assumed was meant as a private space for her, she spied a spacious bedroom with a queen bed and an en suite bathroom. This space was larger than her apartment in New Orleans.

She made her way into the room, tossed her suitcase up on the bed, and proceeded to unpack. The girls stood around the room, silently watching.

"Where are you from?" Lachlyn asked.

"I've moved a lot, but I lived in Scotland until I was fifteen." The source of her slight brogue.

"How many families have you nannied for?" Chloe asked now. Only Rowan caught the searching glance the girl sent her. Was intuition this girl's gift?

Rather than answer her, Rowan turned it back. "How many nannies have you had?"

Lachlyn's lips pinched. "You are the seventh. The first one lasted until we turned five. The other six have been since then."

Rowan paused in hanging up a shirt and raised her eyebrows. "Why so many?"

The girls exchanged a glance, and Lachlyn shrugged. "They didn't like it here."

The smugness in their shared look said it all. They'd run off their nannies. Jeez, they were young to be doing that. But why?

As she reached for another shirt to hang, a black and white cat jumped up on the bed and rubbed against her outstretched hand. Rowan smiled. "Hello there."

The cat nuzzled her hand again.

"Aren't you a queen among felines."

In response the cat curled up beside her suitcase and set to purring with a loud rumble.

"Her name is Nefertiti," Atleigh asked. "She doesn't like people since Grandma Essie died. Dad says."

"I didn't know your grandmother had passed away. That should have been in your file."

"Great-grandmother," Chloe corrected. "We didn't know her."

Rowan looked closer. How old was this cat? A sudden chill passed over Rowan, sending an involuntary shiver across her skin—there, then gone.

"Do you speak with animals?" Atleigh asked.

Rowan stilled. *Dragonfly wings and barnacle butts.* The idea was not to give away her true abilities that could help Greyson identify her.

"I have a slight ability."

"What is your gift?"

"I have no particular gift." True. She possessed many.

Chloe elbowed her sister. "She wouldn't be a nanny if she was fully gifted," she hissed.

"I guess." Lachlyn's suspicion reflected in her narrow-eyed gaze. "You stopped our spells pretty easily."

Rowan continued to unpack. "My skills lend toward raising magical children. Not too difficult. I'm surprised Mr.

Masters didn't stop you himself."

"Using magic against other witches is against the rules," Chloe said.

"And Dad is all about the rules," Atleigh tacked on.

"Ah. I guess this is a good time to discuss *my* rules."

All three groaned, and Rowan held in a grin as she zipped up her suitcase and stashed it in the large closet.

She turned to the girls, hands on her hips.

"I expect you to call me Rowan. I expect responsible magic use, which I did not see today. I expect you to know that if you need something, you can always ask me."

Given the wary gazes aimed her way, Rowan felt it a safe bet none of the other nannies had said anything similar.

"We don't need a nanny," Atleigh said. "We're big girls."

The old souls staring at her from young eyes about broke her heart. These girls needed love. Lots of love. Rowan nodded her head slowly, as if considering that statement. "Fine. Then I'll be chauffeur, cook, and helper when you need it."

"A nanny," Lachlyn grumbled.

Rowan could have spelled them, forcing their compliance or opening their hearts, but she'd much rather earn their trust.

Besides, she needed to reserve her energy for their father. For now.

Chapter Three

Greyson shut the door to his office with a sigh of relief, followed by a flash of guilt. He loved his daughters with every cell in his body, but, even after ten years without his wife, he still had no idea how to deal with three little girls. He had to admit his position as lead hunter for the Covens Syndicate had not remotely prepared him for wrangling with three tiny females. Of course, based on six previous nannies' performances, the girls were a handful for anyone, a fact which made him feel marginally better.

A mental image of the latest in a long line of nannies popped into his mind—creamy skin, wide dove-gray eyes, red curls everywhere, the most adorable freckles. Unbidden, his body hardened. Because of freckles.

"Damn," he muttered.

He'd raised his hands, ready to defend his daughters when Rowan had appeared as if conjured and frozen like an ice cube at the north pole. Those wide gray eyes looking at him in wary interest caught his attention first, followed by the freckles across the bridge of her nose, stark against her pale skin. Angel kisses, he remembered his mother saying about her own freckles when he was a boy. If Rowan had stood closer, he might even have reached out and brushed a fingertip against them. Lust had inconveniently roared through his veins, hitting him like a bolt of lightning on a clear day. Out of the fucking blue. He'd never responded so strongly to a woman. Ever. Not even to his sweet wife.

Guilt twisted inside him like a snake writhing in the grasp of a raptor's talons.

Discovering Rowan was his nanny had been like being dunked in a frigid mountain stream—inappropriate. Wrong on more than one level.

Then she'd opened her mouth, and, rather than the meek and mild woman he expected—like every other nanny sent to him—sass had flowed out from between those pouty lips.

Helpful. He'd had a hard time not laughing at that one, his amusement in the midst of everything else only serving to add to growing frustration with himself. What was wrong with him?

And what was with that strange spark of electricity when he shook her hand? Living in the mountains, he could put it down to static charge, but that bolt felt stronger, sharper. A glance at his palm—which still tingled from the contact, even now—showed no mark. He closed his hand in a fist, then chided himself for being stupid to even look. Of course, that had been static electricity or residual power from the energy balls he'd formed, perhaps—simple.

Greyson reluctantly admitted he'd bolted. He'd had no intention of working today until Rowan McAuliffe had shown up.

The way she'd taken over... *I shouldn't feel so relieved.*

But he had. Like suddenly he wasn't the only one struggling on his own with a whole lot of problems.

A different pang of guilt mixed in with the other

emotions like a tossed salad. His...*attraction* to her had to be an aberration. The girls had been fighting. Again. As usual, he had no idea how to deescalate the situation. His emotions already heightened, he doubted he'd react the same way to Rowan when in his usual controlled state.

Having satisfactorily explained away his odd behavior, Greyson decided he might as well get work done while he was in here. He'd give his nanny time to get settled before he tested her out.

He crossed the small office to sit behind the old pine desk, a wall of bookshelves at his back. Natural light poured in from a set of double doors, which led out to a small side patio. Greyson flipped open the lid of his laptop and logged in. After a couple of clicks, he brought up the file for his latest assignment.

Unfortunately, the case had come to a screeching halt before it ever got started. For the thousandth time, he reviewed the information available.

They'd had two grave abuses of magic instigated by the same creature. Kaios, an ancient werewolf, now deceased, had first employed a warlock to attack a group of nymphs not far from where Greyson lived. With the help of a demigod, the warlock had been captured and held by the nymphs.

The Covens Syndicate had dispatched a different hunter to bring the man in for questioning. But Greyson knew the warlock personally, had history with him, and knew that this wouldn't be the last time he attacked innocents.

He'd taken it upon himself to enact a different penalty—death.

Usually, Greyson refused to mete out that kind of punishment. Banishment, removal of powers—those he could do. But death? Such an act scarred the soul. However, in this particular case, he'd disagreed strongly with the Syndicate's decision to question first and then decide. He'd killed that warlock against their direct orders.

Nothing could have stopped him.

Not long afterward, the same werewolf had attacked Castor Dioskouri, the demigod who'd captured the warlock, as well as Lyleia Nyaid, a nymph and now Dioskouri's wife. That time, though, Kaios had used a witch to turn off their powers. Only by luck and good planning had the Banes and Canis packs of wolf shifters been there to help. Otherwise, Greyson suspected a feud between shifters and gods would have been the result. Kaios had been killed, but his witch accomplice had survived.

Or so Greyson was led to believe.

The Covens Syndicate had dispatched him to deal with the witch in the situation, but she'd disappeared. No one was talking, including the demigod and nymph who'd been attacked, almost as though they were protecting her. Why would they do that?

At this point, all he had to go on was a physical description, a woman, long red hair, green eyes, or maybe gray, not tall but not short, either. Unfortunately, the description fit many witches. Unlike the rest of the world's population, the red-haired gene cropped up almost 50 percent of the time in those magically inclined. Hell, the new nanny now living under his roof matched that description.

But he knew her background. After the sixth failed nanny provided by his community of mages, he'd turned to Brimstone for help. Delilah had provided a full dossier on Rowan's background and skills. No picture, though. That might've been helpful to avoid his reaction today.

And how was a person of ten minutes' acquaintance already distracting him?

With concentrated effort, he focused on the witch he was hunting. The Syndicate's directive so far was to find her and bring her in for questioning. The impression that the witch had performed her magic unwillingly was the only thing keeping Greyson from immediately considering the same punishment he'd given Kaios's warlock: death.

First, he had to find her.

Greyson picked up his cell phone and searched for a number he'd already tried several times. After dialing he waited through several rings, already composing his message in his head when a woman answered.

"Hello?"

"Lyleia Nyaid?"

"Yes. I'm sorry I haven't returned your calls before now, Mr. Masters. Castor and I were on our honeymoon."

His suspicion that all witnesses were avoiding him dulled somewhat, though he didn't dismiss that gut instinct completely. "Congratulations."

"Thank you."

"Rather than take your time now, I was hoping to set up a meeting with you and your…husband next week to discuss the witch involved in the attack."

"Of course. Let me check our calendars, and I'll get back to you on Monday morning."

That's right, she was Dioskouri's executive assistant. Idly, Greyson wondered if that would continue now that they'd married, not that it mattered to him. "Sounds good."

"If you don't mind, I'll include Tala and Marrok Canis-Banes? They are the alphas of the two packs of wolf shifters involved in the fight on our side and might be able to provide more information."

Greyson sat up straighter. After several months of getting the runaround from all parties involved, suddenly this offer seemed too…accommodating. "That would be very helpful. Thank you."

"My pleasure. I hope we can be of help."

"I do, too."

After hanging up with Lyleia, Greyson stared at his phone. Something about this entire situation felt off, wrong. Those involved weren't behaving like experience had taught him to expect.

He'd get to the truth eventually.

Blowing out a frustrated breath, Greyson closed the file on the witch. There was nothing he could do until he'd talked more with the demigod, nymph, and wolf shifters.

"Show me Rowan." With a wave of his hand, the screen of his laptop came to life, showing his new nanny.

Time to see how she handled disaster. Greyson found a person's true personality came out when everything went wrong. He'd put all the previous nannies to similar tests, though he had to admit, curiosity spiked inside him as he wondered how Rowan would react to the challenges he was about to put her through.

Then he'd know if he'd keep her around or not. He ignored the sickening drop to his stomach at the idea of having to turn her away. Her slenderness struck him as unnatural, gaunt almost. But he wasn't in the business of saving strays. The important thing was finding the right nanny for his girls.

Would Rowan prove to be that person?

Chapter Four

The pungent odor of burning reached Rowan's nose, which she wrinkled in distaste as she sniffed the air.

"What in the name of mystical—"

With a gasp she leaped up from the lounger on the back porch, where she was watching the girls practice small bits of magic as they played in the untamed woods behind the house. Silly things like turning a rock into a flower. Now, she turned her back on her charges and rushed into the house and straight for the kitchen.

"No, no, no," she muttered under her breath. She couldn't have got this wrong already.

Sure enough, the charred lump she pulled from the oven in no way resembled food. "My lasagna," she wailed.

With hectic movements, she turned off the oven, turned on the overhead fan, and then opened a bunch of windows.

That'll teach me to try to cook without magic. She tossed a glare at the offending hunk of what had been noodles and sauce. What had she done wrong? Worse, any second Greyson would appear, demanding to know what had happened. No way could he miss the heavy scent of smoke pervading the house.

But after a few minutes, he didn't show. What to do? She could use magic to clear the air and fix the dinner, but would he notice? He was, after all, a powerful mage, and a hunter, which meant he paid attention to details, or he'd never track down those he was after. Technically, using magic to make dinner wasn't a bad thing, but if she showed too many skills, he'd start to ask questions. Nannies' skills were supposed to be domestic, though. Rowan had almost convinced herself to risk it. The alternative was admitting she'd messed up dinner.

Maybe I can start another dish instead? She moved to the pantry, which she'd already snooped around in, and came up with a few cans of tuna. She knew the fridge wasn't much better stocked. *Tuna surprise it is, then.*

Twenty minutes later, a new casserole bubbled away in the oven. So maybe she put a tiny spell on it to ensure it wouldn't burn. Plus, she made sure to check on it often. In the meantime she found a can of aerosol scent and sprayed it liberally throughout the kitchen, leaving the windows open.

At least the weather cooperated, a light breeze blowing through the house and across her skin. Surprisingly mild for November in the mountains, though she was sure, based on the small piles of snow around the bases of the trees, that harsher weather would return soon. Delilah had told her the weather here could change in the blink of an eye. Blizzard one day, melted the next, and back to dry the day after.

A relieved sigh escaped her lips. Greyson hadn't discovered her mistake. Score one for the underdog. The quiet suddenly made itself felt. Darkness had fallen. She should've had the girls inside ages ago. Grabbing her thick jacket, which she'd thrown on the floor earlier, she slipped out to the back patio. All thoughts of dinner vanished as she noted the silence outside. Her steps slowed as she scanned the woods. Where were the girls?

They must've come back inside while I was busy with dinner. However, a quick but thorough check of the house showed her they had not. Rowan refused to allow panic to enter the situation. No way could she have messed up dinner and lost her charges all in the same night. Greyson would fire her on the spot, and then how would she implement her plan?

With hurried steps she went to where she'd last seen the girls. Stopping there, she ran her gaze along the woods, which, after about fifty feet, veered steeply up the side of the mountain. No sounds of laughter or chatter reached her. Where on earth could they be?

A prickle crawled up her neck, and she swiped at it with her hand before she could stop herself.

You're not being watched anymore, she told herself in her best inner stern voice.

She hoped.

Shaking off her apprehension, she assessed the situation. Dinner would be ready soon, under the wire for Greyson's seven o'clock deadline. Magic might be her only option now. Rowan bit her lip. So many spells in one day, of varying kinds, not a great start to flying under the radar. If she could keep it small, maybe they wouldn't realize. Back turned to the house, just in case, she closed her eyes. "*Nuru il immaru.*"

Roughly translated, the words meant to see the light. She thought the words, not daring to say them aloud. The spell would be minimized without the spoken phrases. Exactly as she intended.

With a spell such as this one, she was never entirely sure of the results, leaving the specifics up to the magic. Slowly opening her eyes, she sucked in a breath. Before her a glittering set of golden footsteps wound around the yard. A quick glance revealed the path moving back into the house. So they *were* inside, in one of the few places she hadn't checked, which meant either the attic, Greyson's office, or his bedroom. Had they hidden from her?

Damn, and I thought I was doing so well connecting with them.

Before her spell could fade, Rowan traced their steps back inside to discover the attic had been their final destination. She doubted they'd missed the stench of the smoke from her ruined dinner as they came inside. What if a real fire had blazed and they'd been trapped? And what was their goal by hiding?

Getting her in trouble, most likely.

• • •

Greyson glanced away from his email at the clock in the bottom right corner of his computer screen. Time to go to dinner and see how Rowan had dealt. So far, she'd been a damn sight more enjoyable to watch than the previous nannies. Beyond a small wail of frustration, she'd handled the dinner disaster with compunction, though he'd been mildly surprised she couldn't prepare dinner with magic as the other nannies had. It must not be one of her gifts, which gave him a small sting of guilt for ruining her first attempt and causing her more work.

She moved with a lithe grace, her jeans hugging her backside in a way he couldn't fail to acknowledge. With a grunt he pushed aside any notice of her as a woman and tried to focus on her actions. She'd frantically searched for the girls, then paused at the edge of the woods. No words had been spoken, but with deliberate direction, she'd walked straight to the attic door.

Once there, she'd cocked her head and crossed her arms, frustration pinching her lips. Had she figured out where the girls were hiding? They did this to every nanny, and he allowed it as part of their family test.

"So that's how it's going to be," she finally said, then spun on her heels and returned to the kitchen.

Interesting reaction. Was she going to do anything about her charges being up in the attic?

The dinnertime hour had arrived, which meant he'd discover the answer to his question shortly. He flipped the lid closed on his computer and went in search of a witch. One who'd occupied more of his day than she should've. He entered the dining room promptly at seven to find the table laid for five. A basket of crusty bread and a leafy spinach salad sat in the middle.

"I'll be right there." Rowan's voice drifted to him from the kitchen, but he couldn't see her over the countertops.

Then she stood from where she'd been bent over to remove her casserole from the oven. Unbidden, an image of those jeans stretched tautly over her nicely rounded ass entered his mind. With effort, he pushed it away.

Hands in oven mitts to protect her skin from the piping hot casserole dish, Rowan skirted the large island and entered the room where he waited. She placed the dish on a trivet and removed her mitts, setting them on the corner of the table. Never once looking in his direction, she took a seat. "Shall we?"

His best poker face firmly in place, Greyson also took a seat directly across from her at the long end of the table. Curiosity about her next actions had him firmly in thrall. He glanced behind her in the direction of the attic.

"Would you pass me your plate, please?"

He shifted his gaze to find her holding her hand out patiently. Without a word he meekly passed his plate over. She dished up a healthy portion of whatever she had decided to serve in place of her badly burned lasagna and passed it back.

"Where are the girls?" he asked.

"Hiding." She spoke bluntly and to the point, but no censure or irritation laced her tone.

He cocked his head. "Oh?"

She gave a perfunctory smile, one that didn't appear to reach her eyes, although it was hard to tell, as she had yet to look at him directly, a fact which, perversely, he didn't like. "They'll appear when they get hungry."

"I see." He placed his napkin in his lap and served himself salad before passing her the bowl. "I must say, I'm impressed."

"Why?" Finally, she met his gaze. "Tuna surprise is hardly a gourmet meal."

A chuckle threatened. He hadn't even tasted the casserole yet. "I mean about the girls. Several of my nannies haven't lasted the first night." He shook his head, making his disdain for those other nannies clear. "How hard is it to cook a meal and keep track of three young witches?"

In response Rowan set down her fork and leaned back, observing him through now narrowed eyes. "I think I see."

Damn. She'd figured him out.

But she didn't say any more. He gave her top marks. None of the others had caught on. As if by mutual agreement, they both tucked into their meals. Strangely, the silence descended not with the heavy weight to produce small talk, but with an inexplicable ease. When was the last time he'd sat with a woman, without talking, and neither felt the need to fill the void with inane chatter?

Almost thirty minutes later, the girls finally put in an appearance. "We're hungry."

Rowan greeted them with a welcoming smile. "Have a seat. There's not much left, and it's probably cold, but you're welcome to eat."

Not much left? They'd had only one helping each.

Greyson glanced at the serving dishes. Sure enough, only about a quarter of the food remained.

Had Rowan just spelled the food to reduce the amount remaining and teach the girls a lesson? If she had, she'd done so in front of him without his seeing or hearing. Not even a fizzle of energy in the room or a flicker of a lightbulb. Apparently, his nanny had untapped depths.

He eyed her speculatively. Tricky.

The girls exchanged a glance, then looked toward him. While he'd allowed their hiding act in the past, he'd never actively condoned it. He gave them no help, keeping his expression neutral.

"This smells good," Atleigh, the peacemaker, tried.

Before Rowan could respond, Lachlyn spoke up. "Didn't you notice we were gone?"

No change in Rowan's pleasant expression. "Yes, I did."

"And you didn't look for us? Aren't you supposed to be all caring and stuff?" Lachlyn scowled, but her bluster didn't hide how truly upset she was.

Rowan paused in spooning a miniscule amount of casserole onto a plate for Atleigh. "If you mean fluttering around like a panicked bird caught in a windstorm searching for you, you'll find that's not my style."

"But you knew where they were?" Greyson asked. He needed to be sure he left his daughters with someone capable. Even if her eyes were an extraordinary shade of gray, like moonlight in a forest, and her berry-ripe lips tempted a taste.

Get your mind off her lips, you ass.

She directed a polite gaze his way, but he caught the anger snapping in their depths all the same. "I assured myself they were safe and in the house. They are old enough to arrive at dinner on time, without prompting."

She sent the girls a sweet smile. "After all...you don't need a nanny. Right?"

Lachlyn, whom he'd mentally dubbed the ringleader almost since birth, tipped up her chin. "Exactly."

"Excellent." Rowan divvied out the remaining food.

"Is this all?" Chloe asked, a mournful droop to her mouth.

"I'm afraid so." Rowan showed zero remorse. In fact… was that a twitch to her mouth?

"Can you at least heat it up?" Lachlyn demanded.

Greyson opened his mouth to rebuke her rude tone, but Rowan beat him to it.

"Arrive to dinner late, eat cold food. You chose to be late. Next time, maybe you'll arrive on time." Rowan nodded as though that closed the discussion, and all three girls, in various stages of anger and shock, shut their mouths and accepted their plates without further debate. Greyson had never seen them so subdued. Then, again, no other nanny had handled today quite as Rowan had, either.

After a quiet, and rather strained, rest of dinner, Rowan wiped her mouth with her napkin and stood. "Girls, you may clear the table and clean up the kitchen before you go to bed."

"What? —" Chloe screeched. She turned to him. "Dad, we never clean the kitchen."

"Then it's about time you start." Rowan's quiet words held steel, and he found himself hoping he never landed on her bad side. Of course, if she used that husky voice in that bossy way with him, he might have to do something about it. Something that involved—

What in the seven hells is wrong with me?

Greyson gave himself a mental shake. Instead, he tried to focus on the scene before him and had to hold in a laugh at the three identical expressions of disgruntled acceptance. He should've called Delilah sooner, because Rowan McAuliffe was exactly the person his family needed.

"I'll check on you in about an hour." Rowan turned to

leave but paused in the doorway. "I wanted to thank all of you."

Greyson sat back and waited.

Rowan smiled warmly. "Each household takes time to settle into and become part of the routine. I can't tell you how much I appreciate your efforts to make my day so warm and welcoming and...special."

Did she just *Sound of Music* his family? It worked. Guilt settled like a granite boulder in his gut. Based on their wide-eyed exchange of glances, the girls were dealing with a similar reaction.

Rowan's smile didn't alter exactly, but suddenly a mischievous glint sparkled from those amazing eyes. "I look forward to repaying your kindness."

He didn't remember Julie Andrews saying anything like that in the movie. With a cheerful nod, Rowan turned and quietly left the room. A whisper would've sounded like a shout in the silence she left in her wake.

"Do you think she meant she'd get even?" Lachlyn asked, breaking the hush that had fallen over them.

He dropped his napkin onto his plate. "I suspect so."

"Is she mad?" Atleigh asked.

"Hard to tell. I'll go talk to her."

He left the girls clearing up and made his way to the basement. He fully expected to find Rowan packing her things. Instead, he discovered her on the couch, feet propped on the coffee table, watching a rerun of an old sitcom.

He paused at the sight of cute, bare toes, tension crawling across his shoulders and up his neck. He rolled his head, trying to ease the muscles. It didn't help. Because of toes.

Freckles and now toes.

"I don't appreciate you threatening my children." Not what he'd planned to say, but he didn't take it back.

She jerked a little at the sound of his voice only to ease

back against the couch, a small smile tipping her lips up on one side. "That wasn't a threat," she said. "Did I pass your little test?"

She'd definitely figured it out. "Yes."

"I don't appreciate being tested that way."

He wouldn't, either, but his children and their needs meant he'd do what he had to. "When did you know?"

"When you didn't comment on the burned smell or the fact that I'd left the girls in the attic. Do you do this to all your nannies?"

He sat on the coffee table in front of her, mostly to get her to put those toes away. On the floor where they belonged. Only, instead, she shifted on the couch to bend her knees to the side, tucked up like a fastidious kitten, toes still perfectly visible. What would she do if he flipped a pillow over them? Probably question his sanity and quit.

What was her question again? Right, the girls and nannies. "Testing nannies is important. Atleigh, Lachlyn, and Chloe are quite...unusual."

He caught the way her eyes lit with curiosity. "I'm not permitted to share more than that. But even if they weren't special, they're still three girls on the cusp of teenage-hood and coming into their magic, and they need the right person minding them."

"Delilah sent you duds before?" Her doubt about that came through loud and clear.

"No. I didn't use Brimstone until now. I thought we could handle this through the witching community. I was wrong."

Surprise-widened eyes told him he'd caught her off guard with the admission.

Greyson grinned. "Yes, I can be wrong."

Her gaze dropped to his mouth, and tension filled the spaces inside him like a curtain of electricity. Awareness, impossible to not call it what it was. Rowan snatched her gaze away, and his head cleared enough for the realization to seep in that he hadn't smiled, truly smiled, since his wife's death. The thought struck hard, and he rubbed at a spot on his chest as his mind transitioned from turned on, to shock, to aggravated at himself in the space of seconds, left buzzing with emotion either way.

Pulling his own gaze away, he cleared his throat. He shouldn't be letting his nanny affect him this way. "I should've guessed Delilah would send me someone more than capable."

"I don't know about that," she muttered under her breath. "So all of it was a test. The burned dinner?"

Greyson grimaced. "Yes."

"The girls running away?"

He nodded.

"What about their fight this morning?"

Another grimace. "That was real."

"And your attitude?"

He frowned. "What attitude?"

She peered at him for a long moment, and Greyson got the uneasy impression she found him wanting somehow.

"Never mind," she murmured. Was she placating him?

"Are the schedule and the expectations for me the same?" she asked.

"Yes." What was wrong with his schedule?

Her mouth pursed, but she nodded. "Fine."

"So you'll stay?" Oddly, Greyson found himself holding his breath for her response. An hour in her company, surrounded by her wildflower and honey scent, and part of him wanted her to stay. So unlike him, he brushed that wayward feeling aside with irritation and waited for her response.

She sighed. "I don't have a choice."

The words, or maybe the way she said them, triggered instinct honed over years of being a hunter. "What does that mean?"

A strong emotion flashed in her eyes. If he had to guess, he would've said panic, but the expression was gone so quickly he couldn't be sure.

Then she offered a sweet smile. "It means you clearly need help. So, yes, I'll stay."

Greyson levered to his feet. He needed help, did he? "I'll be in my room if you need me. Good night, Rowan." Her name felt strange on his lips. Right and wrong at the same time.

"Mr. Masters—" She stopped him at the door, and he swung to face her, eyebrows raised in question.

She didn't bother to get up. "Don't test me like that again."

Or what?

"Remember...observations can go two ways."

Did she just imply she was observing him? Before he could snap out a question, she stood and turned off the TV. "Good night."

Greyson headed back upstairs, coming to terms with a rare experience. He'd been effectively dismissed by a woman who happened to be his girls' nanny. Most women rushed to please him. Rowan practically sprinted in the opposite direction.

Bigger question...why did her contrary reaction turn him on?

Chapter Five

Monday morning dawned early, still dark outside. After almost a week with the Masterses, Rowan had learned the hard way how difficult getting three twelve-year-old girls out of bed could be. Sloths had more speed than those three in the morning. Rowan had been damn tempted to give each a little zap but restrained herself.

How had Greyson been doing this on his own the last few years? After that first one, none of the nannies had lasted long enough to be much help. Given his occupation he had to be gone a lot. Yet while the girls might need a bit more attention, they were still good kids. She had to give the man props for that.

At least the pricklies she'd felt in the woods had been Greyson watching, and not…something else. Someone else.

"Get going, lazy bones," she said out loud. Then flipped off the covers.

Without the help of magic for once, Rowan managed to feed the girls and get them out the door with Greyson on time. She peered out the window to the backyard where he was about to teleport them to school after muttering something at Rowan about an errand before he returned to work from home.

With a word she couldn't hear from where she stood inside, in an instant they were gone. A dusting of snow from last night—the first she'd seen since arriving—swirled and flattened in the wake of the whirlwind caused by their departure.

Is that what I look like when I teleport? More than likely her own version came off much less graceful while in her head she was like, "Nailed it!"

Pushing aside the idle thought, Rowan grabbed a feather duster she'd found hanging in the laundry room. The obviously unused thing had, ironically, collected a coating of dust where it hung. So, as she strode with purpose towards Greyson's office, she whispered an incantation that cleaned it off.

She needed a proper alibi if he discovered her in here.

She paused inside the doorway of his office, taking stock of the room. One of the smallest rooms in the house, she found it cozy with its rustic charm, stacks of books, and big pine desk. The desk had nicks, dings, and scratches all over it, as if it had been well loved through many generations of Masterses. Closing the door behind her, she moved farther inside and ran her hand over the surface of the desk, noting the rough texture of the time-worn wood. A crystal-clear image of Greyson working here came to her. An intimate image, like what a wife might walk in on, and strangely her heart stuttered.

Giving her head a shake, she pushed the seductive image away. "You've got a job to do, girl. Get to it," she muttered.

A quick incantation had the duster going to work on the bookshelves without the aid of human hands. It left a faint trail of glittering sparks as it moved, but they dissipated quickly enough that she wasn't concerned. Meanwhile, she moved around to sit behind Greyson's desk.

Getting into his laptop took a little time, as he'd guarded it with magical wards, though not as many as she would've expected, given his job. Perhaps he assumed no one would contemplate getting this close to him? Still, the wards he *had* bothered with, in addition to regular technological security, took some unraveling.

As soon as she breached the computer's defenses, rather than waste time searching manually, she channeled her energy, pulling from the electricity of the device itself.

"*Amaru* Kaios."

The gathered force left her body with the words. Not traditional words of magic, but words the woman who'd raised her had spoken. Ancient words. Powerful words.

The language of demons and angels.

The spell was essentially a search for any files about Kaios, the werewolf who'd trapped her and used her. Enslaved her, more like.

Greyson was sure to have Kaios's name associated with her in the files, as the reason he hunted her was inextricably linked to the werewolf. If Greyson knew the name of the witch involved—her own name—she wouldn't be his nanny right now. In an instant she had the files laid open before her on the screen.

Rowan stilled at the image of the werewolf who'd compelled her to do terrible things. Quickly she clicked for the next image and blanched. The pricklies hit her neck hard, chasing themselves down her back.

The woman from her memories. The one who'd been there any time Kaios hadn't been around, had taunted Rowan with what they'd do with her. As though she'd been thrilled a witch was under this kind of control.

Rowan racked hazy memories of her time with him, when

her mind hadn't entirely been her own, of the fight when he'd been killed. Had the woman been there?

She couldn't remember.

But he'd brought all his followers to that fight. No doubt the woman was in chains or dead.

With a physical shimmy, Rowan shook off the memories. Kaios and his people weren't a threat to her anymore. What she *needed* to focus on was Greyson Masters and the Covens Syndicate.

She read with hungry eyes, searching for any opportunities to plant false clues. The good news was he didn't have much.

"So you already tried to follow my magical trail," she murmured.

He'd had no luck with it. Magic use left a trail of energy that a powerful mage like Greyson could track, depending on how long ago the spells had been cast. According to the files, any magical trail she'd left had disappeared in the woods just outside where the fight had occurred. Spent and scared, she'd had nothing to do with hiding it, which probably meant Delilah had taken care of it.

I'll have to thank her next time I talk to her.

Greyson couldn't scry for her until he had more information or a personal item. The more she read, the more weight the elephant that had been sitting on her chest seemed to lose. Greyson had nothing on her.

Fabulous. Now to keep it that way.

The satisfied smile curling her lips froze as she hit his last entry of notes.

Hell and hexation. He'd been in touch with Lyleia Nyaid and was arranging to meet the nymph along with her demigod husband and the two wolf shifter alphas involved in the fight soon—this week. It looked as if he was waiting on Lyleia to call and arrange the logistics.

If she could get near his cell phone before that call came

through, she could slow things down, at least.

A ripple of energy fluttered across her arms, like a warm spring breeze caressing her skin—her only warning Greyson had returned home. Damn, that was fast. What happened to that errand?

Thankful she'd set up a spell to advise her of his presence, Rowan quickly closed the files, replaced the wards on the computer, and shut it down.

Then she jumped up and grabbed the duster, removing her incantation on it with a whispered word. Just in time, the sparks of magic faded, before the click of the door had her turning, arm raised as though she'd been cleaning all along.

Greyson froze when he spotted her there, a scowl replacing his taken-aback expression. "What are you doing in here?"

He'd been checking the screen of his cell phone when he walked in. Now, as he waited for her answer, he slipped it into the pocket of his black trousers.

Rowan swished the duster. "Cleaning."

When he showed no sign of either moving or talking again, she shifted on her feet. "I was trying to finish before you needed the office. I can come back later."

She went to scoot past where he still stood in the doorway, slowing as she neared, pretending to lower her eyes in subordination, but fixated on the cell phone in his pocket. Focusing her energy once again, she directed all her intent to the device. She'd have to limit the words to her mind, reducing the efficacy of the spell, but it would have to do.

Awatum Suqammumu Balum, Halqu Ina. Translation… words silent without, lost within.

A paper on his desk rustled as the magic left her body. Thankfully, the evidence could be attributed to her walking by. She hoped the magic worked as intended, silencing the device when calls came in and losing the voicemail if any were left. The language she used was Sumerian, created before things like cell phones, ringtones, and voicemail existed, making the terminology she chose a challenge. Dealing with technology in the magic she'd been taught was always tricky.

Her spell cast in the few steps it took to approach Greyson, she continued on her path past him, only to jerk to a stop as he grabbed her wrist.

"Not yet," he said.

Had he felt the ripple of energy, minute as it'd been, or caught the direction of her stare?

The strange spot on her wrist where he'd shocked her the day they met had stopped tingling by that night, but now it started heating again at his touch. Holding in a gasp as warmth spread from the spot throughout her body, she tipped her chin up, looking him directly in the eyes, dark eyes, currently laser-focused on her in a way she didn't entirely trust. He didn't let her go, his large hand wrapped loosely around her now-burning wrist. Did he not feel that?

"My office is off-limits. So is my room, while we're at it."

Relief that she'd not been caught whooshed through her even as his commanding tone put her back up. She just barely kept from rolling her eyes. This was not the army. This was a household, mister.

But she was the nanny, the employee. And she needed to get out of here. Schooling her features into what she hoped was her meekest expression, meek not exactly coming naturally to her, she nodded. "Of course."

She went to leave again, only to have him tug her back.

"And you don't clean. I have a maid who comes in every other week to do that."

Irritation shot through her, though it didn't assuage the heat now spreading from her arm, gathering low in her belly and rippling over her skin. "Any suggestions on what I do with my time?"

Greyson's expressive brows drew together. "What do you mean?"

Was he really that clueless? Most people didn't enjoy hours of sitting around doing nothing. Rowan'd had enough of that over the last year of imprisonment and recent hiding to last a lifetime. No way was she sitting on her ass doing nothing all day.

Eyes narrowed, she stepped closer in to him. Not quite touching, but the heat on her skin now came from Greyson as well as the throbbing spot on her arm, adding to her irritation. "What did the other nannies do during the day while the girls were at school?"

He gave a puzzled shrug. "How should I know?"

"So those poor women sat around idly for eight hours every day just waiting?" She made it clear what she thought of that situation and his part in it.

His jaw hardened, mouth going flat. "I don't appreciate your tone, Rowan."

"I don't appreciate being stuck somewhere with only a TV for entertainment, Grey." His shortened name slipped from her lips and felt good to say—strangely so.

"So that's what you think about my home? That you're stuck in the middle of nowhere?"

A sliver of hurt lined the offended tone of his voice and gave Rowan a pause in her anger. Did he want her to like his home? In actual fact, she adored it. If she'd created a dream home, it would've looked something like this cabin in its idyllic setting.

Cursing her hasty temper and provoking words, and thinking only of healing a minor hurt, she placed her hand on his chest. "No. I love your cabin."

Beneath her palm his heart beat hard, echoing her own tripping heart rate. The spot on her wrist burned just on the edge of pain now, like holding a finger over a flame for too long. Grey said nothing, his expression inscrutable as he stared at her for an interminable moment. Rowan found herself holding her breath.

Then, as if he couldn't resist, he reached up and brushed a finger down her jawline, leaving a trail of sensation in the wake of his touch. His head dipped lower, and Rowan leaned in toward him, eager for his kiss, only to stumble slightly as he stepped back sharply before making contact.

Feeling as though she'd been shoved under a freezing cold shower, a glance up revealed Grey's expression to be closed off, the desire in his eyes from only seconds before, gone. Had she even seen it? Or had she been deluding herself, lured by the heat pouring through her.

Grey moved away, around to the other side of his desk, putting physical distance between them. "I'll think about what you could do during the day while the girls are gone. For now I suggest getting to know the area and the town nearby."

He sat down, opening his laptop in a clear dismissal, and Rowan, head held high, took the hint and left. As soon as she entered her room, she blew out a long, pent-up breath and glanced down at her wrist, then peered closer. The faint line that appeared the first time he touched her had grown, extending into a swooping, curving design now. Nothing recognizable.

"What in all the realms is that?" she muttered, tracing the line with her finger. She almost expected it to sting at her touch, as it did when Grey touched her. But, beyond the tingling that remained from a moment ago, the mark did nothing.

Had he cursed her? Spelled her? She knew of no spells or curses that left a physical mark like this, not a scar, not a stamp, almost like a half-finished tattoo in white ink.

Rowan leaned her head against her bedroom door. Not for the first time, she wished she could ask Tanya about it. She missed her friend and the steadiest mother figure she'd had in her life. Right up until the day Tanya died at Kaios's hand.

Either way, the fact that Rowan's body practically superheated at Grey's touch was damned inconvenient, a distraction and potential embarrassment she didn't need at best. At worst, it was a complication that could keep her from accomplishing what she'd come here for—protecting her own ass. She doubted they'd punish her for her part in the wolf shifter fight when they learned of how she'd been forced, but in investigating that, they'd discover more about her.

She couldn't have that.

Witches feared demons above all other creatures. Having been raised by one was not information she wanted the Syndicate to discover. In addition, her most powerful gift with animals made her vulnerable to being controlled by werewolves, which, in turn, made her a possible weapon against others, including witches. No way would the Syndicate of the world's covens of witches allow her to live her life in peace once they discovered her secrets—or possibly live at all.

She presented too big a threat. Her existence posed too many questions for comfort.

Hopefully, her spell on Grey's phone would do the trick for now. Her lips hitched in a wicked smile. How long would it be before he figured out he wasn't receiving calls or messages?

Chapter Six

Rowan stared at the ceiling in her bedroom. Painted white and with a fan that wasn't running. In the summer, that probably was handy to have, but not needed in the late fall. Tempting to bewitch the ceiling to show her something—anything—else. Because white paint wasn't exactly stimulating. Unfortunately, it wasn't sleep inducing, either.

Blowing out a long, frustrated breath, she finally gave in, like she did every night, and flipped the covers back. After wrapping a sweater around her, she tiptoed upstairs in her socked feet to the kitchen where she filled a kettle. Leaning her butt against the island counter, she crossed her arms and waited.

The soft, sort of fuzzy, sound of water boiling joined the sound of the ticking grandfather clock in the family room. She couldn't decide if that clock, which faithfully chimed the hour, was her friendly companion or her nemesis. In fact... She glanced over her shoulder. Yup. Another minute or two and it would sound the one o'clock bell.

She turned back to the kettle, cocking her head to listen

to the bubbling, and grinned. This was going to be a close race. Which would go off first? Kettle or clock? Clock or kettle? The telltale click of the hour hand sounded a beat before the clock chimed. Almost a full two seconds later, the kettle started its whistle.

As she quickly removed it from the heat, so the sound wouldn't disturb the other sleeping occupants of the house, she shook her head. "You let a clock beat you?" she asked the kettle. "That was a sad showing. Just like the tortoise and the hare."

"Are you talking to a kettle?" An unmistakable voice sounded from the shadows to her right.

Rowan managed to contain the jump of fright to only her heart. "I—"

Why didn't she get that prickly, being-watched sensation around him?

Greyson's question sank in, and she wrinkled her nose. "Maybe?"

He moved closer to lean a hip against the counter, arms crossed. In pajama pants and a plain black T-shirt, hair all rumpled, suddenly the witch hunter appeared more... accessible.

"Is that a question?" he asked.

She shrugged. "I think any answer might incriminate me, so..."

Turning away, she got down one of the teacups she'd discovered the first night. True teacups—delicate white china with pastel flowers and butterflies painted on them. After a second, she grabbed a second one and lifted it, eyebrows raised in question. "Want some?"

He seemed to hesitate over the answer. "Sure."

With a nod, she set both cups down and then got out a container she'd stashed in the same cupboard and scooped loose leaves into individual silver infusing balls.

"What is it?" Grey asked, suddenly sounding suspicious.

"Chamomile and lavender. In theory it should help make you sleepy. No caffeine."

A glance at his face showed his eyebrows raised. "I don't remember buying that."

"You didn't. I did."

"Oh."

She left the tea steeping in the hot water and turned to face him more fully. "Can't sleep?"

Again, she got the impression that he was hesitating over the answer. "Most nights."

"I haven't bumped into you before." Or heard any sign of his wakefulness. Granted, his room was at the other end of the first floor.

"I didn't want to disturb you."

In other words he didn't want to have to spend time with her. Disappointment dug under her skin and lodged there uncomfortably.

"Not because of what you're thinking," he said.

She blinked. Had she been that obvious?

Her no doubt disgruntled expression must've amused him, because his lips tipped up slightly. "I just didn't want to make you uncomfortable if you were trying to relax."

Sweet. She hadn't expected a witch hunter to be...kind. "I don't mind the company." The words escaped her before she'd realized she wanted to say that. But once the words were out, she didn't want to take them back.

At his inquiring look, she hitched herself up on the countertop, legs dangling. "I've been alone a lot..."

Mother of pearl. What was wrong with her, confessing such a thing? Then another realization struck. Nanny version of Rowan hadn't been alone. She'd been nannying for families. She scrambled to cover her gaff. "Don't get me wrong. The kids are wonderful and entertaining. But it's nice to talk to an adult every once in a while."

There. That sounded plausible and normal.

She glanced at the tea, willing it to steep faster. Why in the seven hells had she confessed such a thing to begin with? Sure, she was lonely all the time. Especially lately. Delilah had turned into a friend of sorts, but not someone to just have a chat with. And she was terrified most of the time. One week here and she was already dreaming of the day she had a home and people to love her. Expecting Grey to care about her at all, as his nanny of all people, let alone the idea of the man hunting her down turning into any kind of friend...

She'd had some dumbass ideas in her time, but this one was a doozy.

"I get it."

His dark voice pulled her out of her head, and she paused, searching his face for any sign of what he meant. "You do?"

Grey huffed a laugh. "I'm a single father with triplet daughters who lives alone in the woods. My job keeps me out on my own for days or weeks at a time. But when I come home, I'm Daddy. Yeah. I get it."

Something in the way he looked down at his bare feet caught her attention.

"Admitting you're lonely even with your children to care for isn't wrong. You know that, don't you?"

He slowly raised his head to stare at her more closely. "In my head I do." His lips hitched in a crooked smile that shot straight through her. "My heart is a different matter."

Rowan curled her hands around the lip of the granite countertop to keep from reaching out to him. "Anyone can see how much you love those girls."

No answer.

Rowan tried a teasing grin. "Even if your daily schedule sounds like it comes from a military drill sergeant."

That earned her a scowl and the return of the forbidding

guy from day one.

Damn. As usual, she'd let her tongue take it a step too far.

Only she couldn't find it in herself to be intimidated. Self-preservation said she should, but he reminded her of Tanya this way. Every so often her adoptive mother's inner demonic self would take over, her temper rising, and she'd suddenly change. Greyson was like that. Like an inner demon drove him beyond his limits.

Rowan imagined he'd look this way in full hunter mode when taking down a witch or warlock who'd earned a harsh punishment. In control, formidable, all consuming.

Entrancing.

If she wasn't likely to end up on the wrong end of his magic, she'd find him fascinating rather than terrifying. Almost as though, if she leaned into that darkness, she'd find...

What? A kindred soul?

Rowan gave herself a mental palm to the forehead. *What am I thinking?*

· · ·

Damn Rowan and damn his instinct to come in here in the first place. He'd leave, only he still had to drink his tea.

Meanwhile, the witch who was his children's nanny, seemed hell-bent on never reacting the way he would expect.

He'd been drawn out here by a small sound to find her talking to the teapot as though it had been in a race with the clock. With anyone else, he'd be on the phone voicing his concerns to Delilah. But he hadn't because something about Rowan—something that had been bugging him all week— hinted at an emptiness. As if she had this void of need that went so deep, she couldn't see the bottom.

He knew that kind of ache. Alone in a crowd.

So he'd tried to offer a bit of compassion. He definitely wasn't expecting her to turn it back on him and see beneath his own words of comfort to the guilt that ate away at him for being almost relieved when he got to go out into the world. Not that he ever wanted to leave his children. But being able to focus on problems outside their home, and have adult conversations, and not be tied to that schedule, was a break he needed.

And his nanny was the only one to see that about him. Not even his own mother knew. Maybe because Rowan recognized her own loneliness in him?

But then, just as he was warming up to her, Rowan was calling him a drill sergeant when it came to his children and they were back to square one, with him gritting his teeth.

"I find a schedule and consistency helps," he said.

And held in a mental grimace. Now he sounded defensive and like a studious professor all at the same time.

"You're right, of course." She ducked her head, but he still caught the smile she tried to hide.

Irritation bubbled up like that teakettle over the fire. "Now you're placating me."

"Not at all." She shook her head, her red curls spilling over her shoulders. "This is a sensitive subject. We can talk about something else."

"I'm not sensitive—"

"It's okay. Every parent has a different way. It's whatever works for you. Right?" She hopped off the counter and fiddled with their cups, removing the silver balls full of the leaves and cleaning them out. "I mean, it's what gets you from one day to the next that counts."

Greyson struggled to find a reasonable response to that. Somehow, she'd managed to make his being both a drill sergeant and sensitive okay. For a woman with minimal magical abilities, Rowan was a witch in every other sense of the word.

But out of all that, what caught him on the raw was the last bit. "Is that how you feel? Just getting from one day to the next?"

Her hands stilled and then moved slightly faster as if she'd paused and then jumped ahead a beat. "Not when I'm with the girls. But...yeah."

"Why?"

What on earth could be that hard in a nanny's life?

She shrugged. "I imagine having a set place in this life is something you've always known. Taken for granted even."

A set place?

As though she'd heard the question, she nodded. "You come from a long magical line that guarantees your position in society. Your abilities grant you automatic respect. People listen to you, don't they? You have family to love and care for you. Not just the girls but others, even if they're not immediately here."

She turned and handed him his teacup, but she refused to look at him. And she was careful not to touch him, offering the cup with the handle facing him.

"I don't see—"

"You have this house—" She waved around with her free hand. "Roots. Family. Love. A set place in life."

"And you don't?"

The smile that came and went was more resigned than amused. "I definitely do not."

Greyson opened his mouth. He wanted to argue with her. To tell her she was wrong. But not because of the need to be right, more out of a need to make her not right. To take that kind of pain away somehow. Fix it for her.

Only he couldn't.

Even if she stayed until the girls were old enough not to

need a nanny, she'd only be here a few years at most, and then off to her next posting.

"Even a set place in life doesn't mean you have no problems." Now where had that come from?

Rowan tipped her head, something in her gaze turning compassionate. "That was insensitive of me. Your wife?"

For once, the pain surrounding Maddie's death didn't jump at him, more like a dull throb. "That. And other things." Like the girls and the questions surrounding their powers. "Being a hunter isn't exactly safe."

He wasn't sure what he expected her reaction to be, but a scowl swiftly smoothed over wasn't it. "I don't suppose it would be," she said slowly. "Why keep doing it then?"

A question he'd asked himself more and more lately.

"Family expectations, at least that's how it started. My family line has been hunters going back generations. I was proud to carry on the tradition of upholding the laws, keeping our people safe from illegal use of magic and the impacts that can have. I'm good at it." Usually. Not lately.

"Sounds like there's more to it."

He blinked. How did she do that? See through him and beyond his words. "Until recently, I've been hunting down a...witch killer." *I shouldn't be telling her this. She'll hate me if she finds out I executed the bastard in cold blood.* "I can't say more than that."

"Of course." She held up both hands then smiled, but not a real one. More like she'd had to pin this one back in place. As though she'd chased away her own demons.

Now I'm seeing things. Greyson shook off the odd thoughts. He didn't need her understanding, and she didn't need his help.

Or maybe that was what she wanted him to think. It seemed to him that Rowan McAuliffe was the last woman to appreciate pity or charity.

Just for something to do, he lifted his cup and took a sip. Immediately a lovely warmth spread through his muscles, relaxing the bunching muscles along his shoulders.

He stared at the pale liquid in one of the dainty cups his wife had insisted they have in the house. "You said this was chamomile and lavender?"

"Mm-hmm." She said around her own sip. Then sent him a smile.

"No magic?"

"No." She pulled a face that he would have described as disgusted. Except that made no sense.

"Well it works, whatever it is. I feel more relaxed already."

That drew a chuckle from her. "My mother used to make this for me."

"Have you always had trouble sleeping? Usually that's a mark of a powerful mage, but—" He cut himself off as his own perceptions and prejudices became more real than he liked to admit.

"But someone like me?"

Damn. He'd offended her anyway.

"I didn't mean—"

Rowan shook her head. "It's okay. I get that…a lot." She tossed him a wave and a casual smile that didn't get anywhere near those silvery eyes. "I'd better say goodnight."

"Night—" He called after her departing form.

He should probably go to bed himself. Maybe the tea would actually bring sleep. The dark certainly didn't. It only brought thoughts and doubts and more worries.

"Smooth move," he muttered at his teacup. Then downed the rest and went to check on the girls before returning to his bed.

Only, when his head hit the pillow, he felt a tiny bit less alone than he had before he'd joined Rowan in the kitchen, and sleep came quickly.

Chapter Seven

Rowan had no idea what she was expecting after the middle of the night moment with Grey. After all, it was just a cup of tea, and she was just his nanny. But somewhere between falling instantly asleep and getting the girls up and ready, she'd convinced herself that last night had to be nothing.

Only she'd been rattled. By his admission that he had problems, too. By the pain in his eyes when she'd brought up his wife. By the way he'd talked about his job as something good for the magical community. He believed that.

But she still shouldn't trust him. This man had been ordered to hunt her down.

So beyond taking care of his children, her only concern needed to be getting in the way of his investigation and keeping her secrets. Beyond that, keeping her distance was for the best.

Luckily, most of the day she'd managed to stick to that, and Grey seemed to have come to the same conclusion.

That part stung more than she wanted it to. This morning, the girls had been halfway through the scrambled eggs and toast she'd made for breakfast, backpacks already sitting by the door ready to go, when he'd walked in.

Damn, the man could fill out a suit.

Why he insisted on wearing more formal clothing when he was working from home, she had no idea. But, overlaid in her mind, was the image of him rumpled and more casual, and sexy as hell, in his pajamas.

He almost felt out of place to her now in the suit. Like he was hiding the real him. A fanciful thought she mentally smacked down.

He'd completely ignored her beyond a coldly cordial nod of acknowledgment.

"Ready?" he'd asked the girls.

In the usual flurry of last-minute things to grab, he'd managed to get them out of the house. And Rowan had stood in the center of the kitchen frowning after their departing backs and the sudden, strange urge to go with him to drop the girls off. She had no right to want things like that.

No matter what, he was still just her boss.

And the witch hunter after you, she'd mentally berated herself. Several times throughout the day, if she was honest.

Between avoiding him and her own mental peppering of good common sense where he and the girls were concerned, she'd managed to keep her distance all the way through dinner. It helped that Grey had kept his conversation limited to the girls' days. Back to normal for him, it appeared. After which, Rowan had headed down to her basement rooms, ignoring the small frown he'd sent her when she'd stood up. In her room, she had turned on the TV only to sit and stare at it without really absorbing the shows that flickered across the screen.

Just stay out of his way, and make sure he stays out of yours.

Rowan blew a breath through pursed lips. She'd been

doing that a lot lately. As though the tension in her kept blowing her up like a balloon and the only way to release it was to squeeze it from her lungs, one long puff of air at a time.

A glance at the clock told her she'd better check on the girls.

They should be in bed already, but she looked in on them every night. Quietly moving through the house, she tried not to notice the light coming from under Grey's office door. With a quiet click, she checked Lachlyn's room first, but found the bed empty. A soft murmur of voices came from the last room, a bigger room created to be more of a playroom for the girls. Though they were almost too old to play in there.

Rowan made a mental note to ask Grey if she could convert it into a teen room with things they'd like. Atleigh was a gamer, so a setup in there might be cool. Chloe loved crafts, so maybe a table and drawers filled with things like that. And Lachlyn was the reader of the three. So a nook with shelves and cushions could be just what she'd love.

Rowan paused outside the entrance to the room, frowning at herself. *Now how did I know all that about them? It's hardly been any time at all.*

"We should go to bed," Lachlyn's voice caught her attention. "Rowan will be up any minute."

That made her smile. At least she was doing that consistent thing Grey insisted was important.

"If she catches us awake, she'll probably want to do something like read us a story," Chloe said.

"Like we're still little girls." Rowan couldn't see them around the corner but could just picture Atleigh's roll of her eyes.

With a grin and a shake of her head, she popped into the room. "Too late."

Shocked open mouths gave way to an exchange of dismayed grimaces that only had Rowan chuckling. "Only I think you'll like my kind of stories."

"We don't *need* a story," Atleigh tossed off.

Rowan grabbed a cushion and plopped down on it, ignoring the way they moved to get up. "Everyone loves a good story. Don't worry. This one isn't for little girls."

Doubt stared back at her from three sets of aquamarine eyes. Lachlyn dropped back to where she'd been leaning against the wall, arms crossed. "Okay."

The other two seemed to take their cues from her and settled as well.

Rowan cleared her throat. "This is a little trick my mother taught me before she died. She used to do this for me every night before bed."

Unimpressed had a look, and it was preteen girls.

"Before I get started, you have to give me a beginning sentence."

Atleigh rolled her eyes again. "I bet you don't have good stories."

"Try me."

The girl narrowed her eyes. Then gave a pouting shrug that would give a diva a run for her money. "Fine." She took an exaggerated breath. "There was a girl misnamed Hope, who…" She left the sentence dangling.

Rowan smiled, then lifted her palm and manifested a small glowing light there. With a whisper of a spell, the glow took the form of a small girl with long blonde hair looking into a pond.

All three girls sat forward, eyes wide.

"Hope guarded a pond deep in the forest into which she poured her own tears. For she'd been gifted with the ability to cure anyone if they drank of the pond of tears."

The glowing form in her palm leaned forward to blink tears into the pond, the surface rippling with each precious drop.

"Only no one had found her in so long, Hope couldn't stand the loneliness. She had no idea what was happening in the world around her. So one day…"

The glowing figure wiped her face and got to her feet.

"…she decided to leave her pond and her forest."

The girls each sat forward now, gazes raptly watching the figure in the woods, the glow casting dancing colors on the walls all around them.

She was taking a risk, revealing this small ability. But it was one that didn't require much power, and if it meant finding a way to connect with these girls…worth it.

"What happens next?" Chloe whispered.

Rowan smiled. "That depends on you. I need another line."

. . .

The late-night tea with Rowan had been a mistake.

He was still clear about that with himself. Keeping a professional distance with her was important for the employee/employer relationship.

But he was starting to realize what having her here could mean for his girls. Greyson stood in the hallway outside the playroom, leaning against the wall, chin to his chest. He watched the play of light on the walls coming from the room and listened to Rowan's lilting cadence as she told his girls a fantastical tale of a girl who changed the world with her tears. She paused every so often to give them a chance to direct the story with her. He had no idea what the lights were but could hazard a guess. A simple spell that a witch of Rowan's level could manage.

At first, he'd been tempted to go in and stop her. What kind of frivolous magical use was that teaching his daughters? But then he'd heard the eager fascination in their voices as they discussed the next lines to give Rowan, and he'd stopped himself.

They sound like themselves.

His heart turned inside out in that moment. For the first time in weeks he heard joy and interest in their voices. Not the pouty, grumbling, resentful version of preteens they'd turned into lately, but his bright, funny, eager daughters.

A series of giggles erupted from the room. He'd missed whatever happened in the story. But he didn't care. The sound of happiness from his babies stole right into his heart. However Delilah had found Rowan, he'd thank her. Because, as unconventional as she seemed with her casual clothes and bare feet and midnight teas and the way she dealt with the girls, she'd somehow managed to do what no other nanny had yet.

She'd made them happy. Even if for a moment.

Hell, he was their *father*, and he hadn't made them laugh like that in longer than he cared to admit. Rowan McAuliffe was worth her weight in gold.

Another reason to keep it professional. No way would he mess up how she worked with his kids. Not if this was the kind of results she got.

Another round of giggles had him smiling, but he could also tell Rowan was coming to the end of her story. With more reluctance than he cared to admit, quickly and quietly, avoiding the third step down that always squeaked, he snuck away. Rather than go to bed himself, he went to his office where he sat down in front of his computer only to stare at the black screen, unseeing.

Rowan McAuliffe, in a short period of time, seemed to be changing everything.

The trouble was there were things she didn't know. One big thing he hadn't shared with Rowan. Hadn't shared with any of the nannies. The reason he'd been up last night for tea had more to do with the girls than he'd let on. No way was he trusting anyone other than himself to deal with it.

For now, he'd keep a close eye, but otherwise let her do her thing.

With a flick of his finger, he turned on his laptop. He'd been in the middle of reading a report when he'd heard Rowan go up and, for some inexplicable reason, decided to follow. But he had work to do. Even at a dead stop, like he was with the witch and werewolf case, he was still working with subordinate hunters on other cases. He had at least five more reports to read and give feedback on before he headed to bed.

He didn't look up until the screen started to blur as his eyeballs protested overuse. Sitting back, he dragged a tired hand over his face, then shut down and went to his room. But the second his head hit the pillow, he knew sleep was going to be elusive again tonight.

Because, despite the heavy lids and sandpaper eyes, his mind would just not shut off. Among a case that had stalled like nothing he'd encountered before, his worries over his girls, trying to be the only parent, and now a red-haired witch whose image wouldn't leave him alone, he was screwed.

A familiar whistling noise coming from the kitchen abruptly cut off. Rowan was in the kitchen making her middle of the night tea again. He frowned at the ceiling fan over his head. Greyson knew exactly why he couldn't sleep but suddenly wondered why she couldn't. What worries could a nanny with no family have?

None of your business.

He managed to force himself to lie in bed another five minutes, determined to ignore the fact that she was in his kitchen right now.

Then, somehow, he was up and down the hall, standing in the shadowed doorway taking in the loose pajama pants

and a shirt with stars on it with the words, "night-night time."
As he watched, she rubbed at her left calf with her right foot.
An easy, unconscious gesture that, for whatever odd reason,
made him want to smile.

Without thinking beyond the moment, he stepped farther
into the kitchen. "Can a guy get in on a cup of that?"

Chapter Eight

A soft sound had Rowan opening her eyes to find her bedroom pitch black. A sound she might've slept through if a sudden chill hadn't skated through her, snapping all her senses awake. A quick glance at the clock on the bedside table told her the time was three in the morning. Blearily, she blinked at the glowing green numbers, even as she pricked her ears for the sound that had woken her in the first place.

It couldn't be Grey. They'd bumped into each other in the kitchen only a few hours ago. A new habit that she had to admit was becoming…addictive.

During the day, they held their distance. Employer and employee. And that was it. He worked in his office. She kept herself occupied during the day and otherwise spent most of her time with the girls. But then at night… At night, they shared a cup of tea and the fact that they both couldn't sleep. Chatted about innocuous things. Okay, maybe for an hour or two. Sometimes. But that didn't mean anything. After all that they simply went to bed.

Nefertiti, Grandma Essie's cat who'd taken to sleeping

with Rowan, lifted her head and twitched her tail, also seeming to listen. They didn't have to wait long. The padded thuds of feet, followed by the faint but distinguishable creak of a floorboard had her up and out of bed, instantly wide awake.

The temptation to use a spell to turn off all powers around her, in case someone was coming for her, itched at her palms, but she resisted. If it came to a fight, she'd pull out that power then, rather than reveal herself now. Waiting was still a risk, as a powerful mage could likely block her before she could get any kind of defensive spell going. However, the niggling doubt this might not be about her meant she had no choice. Her spell to shut down powers sapped her strength more than any other. She'd used it on more than one person only that time with the girls and it had worked only because they were young and inexperienced.

No. She might need her strength to get away.

As quietly as she could without magical help, Rowan snuck up the stairs. Just as she turned to search the kitchen, she caught the beam of a flashlight in the woods out back.

Fantastic.

Just to be sure, a quick check of the girls' rooms confirmed her suspicion. Her charges had snuck out in the middle of the night. But why?

After a trip back down to the basement for boots and a thick jacket—the Colorado mountains at night, even with the mercurial weather in late fall, were freezing, especially with the fresh layer of early snow that had fallen yesterday. Upstairs, she moved to the shelves by the fireplace, shivering as she passed through a cold draft, probably from when the girls had opened the door. Grabbing the flashlight off the shelf, she headed outside.

Using the same spell she'd cast on her first day to track their path, she followed sparkling footsteps up the side of the mountain into the thick wood. About to round a large granite boulder, a large, masculine hand clamped around her mouth. Her assailant grabbed her from behind, his arm wrapping around her stomach. Terror slammed through her system. Heart pounding and adrenaline spiking, she dropped her flashlight and, driven by pure instinct to protect herself, formed sizzling orbs of energy in her hands with a single thought.

At the same time a memory slipped in and claimed her mind, one still fuzzy with the haze she'd been in while under Kaios's control. She'd tried to escape, but someone had found her and dragged her back. Who?

The woman. The one who had hurled horrible words at her. Teasing her about her dead parents and the way Tanya had died and how Rowan would, too, when Kaios was done with her. The spider sensation crawling down the back of her neck turned almost painful.

"It's Greyson," a deep male voice murmured in her ear. "You're okay."

Relief smacked her in the chest so hard, she gasped. She wasn't a prisoner anymore. Kaios was dead. That woman, whoever she was, was dead or captured. *I'm…safe…*

Warmth lit up on her wrist, albeit a little late to keep her from manifesting the damn weapons in her hands.

Immediately the energy, which she had pulled from her own body, dissipated back into her system, leaving her both drained and charged simultaneously. In the same instant, she became horribly aware of the hard length of Grey's body pressed up against her back.

"You won't scream?" he asked.

She shook her head, and slowly he removed his hand from her mouth and turned her to face him, though he didn't step back. She raised her gaze to find him watching her closely, a finger held to his lips.

"You scared the seven hells out of me," she hissed quietly.

"That many?" Amusement crinkled his eyes, visible in the glow of her flashlight, which had fallen with the beam illuminating their feet.

She scowled, not finding him funny in the least.

He leaned forward, lips at her ear. "Sorry. I didn't want you to stop the girls."

Rowan gave an involuntary shudder as his warm breath tickled over her skin. At the same time, she took a mental step back, unable to physically do so, prevented by the boulder at her back. Attraction to Grey equaled bad fucking idea. Instead, she focused her mind elsewhere, on why they were both in the dark woods in the first place.

"Why?" she voiced the obvious question.

"It'll take too long to explain right now. Let's make sure they get back safely. I'll tell you more then."

Rowan nodded and, with a wave of his hand, Grey indicated she should continue to follow the girls. Not too far from where he'd stopped her, they found the triplets in a clearing standing in a perfect circle of aspen trees. The three stood in a column of pure light cast by the full moon, making their blonde hair appear almost silver. Arranged in a circle, hands clasped, eyes closed, they swayed together in a rhythm only they understood.

"What are they do—?"

Grey held his finger up to his lips, then turned back to the scene.

Rowan's mouth dropped in a silent gasp as the three figures started to glow—softly at first, then brighter until the white light became blinding, painful to the point that she could hardly stand to look at them. Meanwhile, silence reigned all around. Even the sounds of the night had ceased—the animals, the breeze through the needles on the pine trees—everything still and quiet, as though the world had hit pause to watch.

Then Chloe's voice sounded from the center of the light. "Rowan McAuliffe. She is here to help us."

Tension seized through her, clenching every muscle hard. Was she about to be unmasked? Then the scar on Rowan's wrist sprang to blistering life at the pronouncement. *What. The. Mother Goddess?*

A glance showed Grey equally stunned. She wasn't sure how she could tell, as his expression remained neutral as ever, but his mouth appeared tighter, his dark eyes wary. What had just happened?

Before she could ask the questions that wanted to tumble off her lips, he took her by the hand and pulled her back to the boulder where he'd stopped her earlier, tugging her around the side. Moments later, as though in a trance, Chloe, Lachlyn, and Atleigh floated past, heading in the direction of the house.

Slowly, she and Grey followed. As they walked, Rowan's mind swirling with questions, she happened to spy a pygmy owl perched in the branches of a tree, watching her. But he didn't say anything as they walked by, so she wrote off his appearance as coincidence. Animals didn't always talk to her.

Once inside the house, they found the three back in their beds, sound asleep. With a jerk of his head, Grey indicated Rowan should follow him. He led her to his office, a room she hadn't revisited since the day he had caught her there.

After only two weeks, she now had trouble picturing Grey in here much, despite the fact that this was where he spent most of his time lately. His demeanor, his physicality, was too big, too vital to be trapped behind a desk. During the day she'd sometimes find him prowling restlessly through the house only to disappear again after he bumped into her. Part of her cheered, knowing his search for her continued to move slowly. But a perverse part of her twanged with guilt at being the cause for his being stuck.

"Please, take a seat," he waved to one of the two leather chairs facing the desk and took the other.

She did so after taking off her jacket. He'd seen her in her comfy peach-colored pajamas often enough at this point. "What just happened?"

Grey ran his hands through his hair, making the dark strands stand on end and suddenly appearing ragged around the edges, not the fully-in-control warlock he usually presented to the world. This was the more human version of him that she encountered each night. Unfortunately. Because she liked this Grey, and right now she needed answers.

"Honestly, I don't know," he said. "They've been doing that since they could walk."

"Sneaking out to…what?"

He shook his head. "They don't sneak. It's more like sleepwalking or a kind of trance. We don't know what they do. I've had them tested, placed spells, and so on. I've brought in the Syndicate to help. All that's been determined is my daughters have a magical connection to some power other than witchcraft. But we don't know who, or what, or if there's a purpose."

Rowan's stomach twisted inside her. In two short weeks, the blonde munchkins had burrowed into her heart like Nefti when the cat burrowed under the covers to sleep at her feet. She couldn't imagine the worry Grey was dealing with. "Do they remember anything when it happens?"

"No."

"Can you stop them from going outside?"

"Yes, but they struggle against the bonds. Chloe has a permanent scar on her leg because of it. I decided the safer option was to follow them, ensuring their protection."

"I'm surprised the cold didn't wake them up." They'd been in pajama pants and tops with slippers on. The slippers had to be soaked by now from the snow.

Then her mind caught up to the situation, which triggered a thought, followed by a swell of anger, like a rogue wave, pushing at everything in its wake. She sat forward, pinning him with a direct look. "And you didn't think to mention this to the woman watching over them?"

The sharp bite to her voice should've been unmistakable, but if he recognized her anger, he gave no indication. "We've shared this information with only a select few. I have a spell cast on their room, so I know when they leave and can follow."

The wave fizzled out, and Rowan sat back in her chair. "I see."

But he still hadn't trusted her. Why she thought she had any right to his trust, she had no idea. Because she damn well didn't, just the same as she could never trust him.

What she should be focused on was how to absorb this new complication? Had Delilah known? "So, you don't know what they meant about me?"

She had yet to check the lines on her wrist. The sharp burning sensation had eased but continued to tingle. However, that could be her proximity to Grey, or the way he'd held her hand, or the false sense of intimacy generated by the small space and the fact that they huddled here together in the middle of the night in their pajamas.

He didn't move, but the light in his eyes changed... shifted. As though he were studying her more closely, but not entirely in a clinical sense. Thanks to her red hair, men often watched her with interest, but this was different. The look struck her like a piano key striking the chord, sending her vibrating.

"I don't have a single clue," he finally said.

Only she didn't believe him. The lack of trust was showing again. He just didn't want to voice what he was thinking. Rowan opened her mouth only to close it again. There didn't seem to be more to say, so she stood. "I'd better get back to bed."

Again, if her abruptness surprised him, Grey didn't express it. He walked with her through the dark and quiet house to the door in the kitchen leading to her stairs. There she turned to face him. Except he was too close, like in the woods, the heat of his body surrounded her. She stepped back, bumping the doorframe, pretending not to see the sudden dance of amusement in his gaze that managed to spark her own irritation. "How often do they go out?"

"Sometimes once a week. They can go as long as a month between."

That often? She frowned. "Since I've been here?"

"This was the second time."

Guilt slowly dripped through her veins. She'd missed them leaving once already. What kind of caregiver did that make her?

And Grey? He got up with them every week like this? *Newts eyes and bats wings.* He had taken on the role as sole nighttime bodyguard, on top of everything else. If he wasn't hunting her down, and constantly keeping secrets from her, she might have let herself appreciate him for the good man he seemed to be.

Maybe she could help. She might have no choice but to submarine his investigation into her, but the part of her starting to connect to him and his family couldn't just look the other way. "Can you expand your alarm to let me know as well?"

He searched her eyes. The woodsy scent of his body, and something more, a manly musk that made her want to bury her face in his neck and inhale, sent the tingling on her wrist to a lick of fire, spreading and sliding over her skin.

"Why would you want that?" he asked slowly.

She did her damndest to ignore the burn. "To help you."

That was way too personal. She cleared her throat and tried again. "As their nanny, it's my job to watch out for them." Mostly true, just not the whole story. "If you don't, I'll just sleep less, worrying and listening, and follow anyway."

Hell, she'd set her own alarm.

"All right." But he didn't leave her, all traces of earlier amusement gone as his eyes turned penetrating.

"What?" she whispered.

But even she knew the answer to that. Any time they were near each other, like their nightly chats, inexplicable, inadvisable tension sat between them like a wall. One that, up till now, neither of them had tried to scale. Only now that wall swelled between them, pressing against her and around her from every direction.

He didn't answer for a long moment, giving a small shake of his head, as if telling himself to stop. "What is it about you?"

Panic fluttered against her chest like a trapped bird. She had to defuse this situation. Now. "I talk back."

Surprised amusement tugged at his lips. "What?"

"I suspect I'm the only woman who's ever argued with you. Am I right?" She couldn't help herself. She argued with him about how they dealt with the girls. Or about the use of magic in the house. Or about trips to the grocery store. Or dinner. Hell. Just last night she'd argued with him about mustard versus mayonnaise-based potato salads. The man had had the temerity to judge her mustard-based concoction at dinner, and she'd declared that if he wanted mayonnaise in his potato salad, he could damn well cook it himself.

Now, rather than backing away, he moved closer. "And?"

She shrugged. "Most people naturally want to be accepted."

"And you don't accept me?" He was laughing at her now. A chuckle had snuck into his voice, a suspicious quiver hovering about his lips.

Kissable lips. Damnable lips.

Given how rarely he smiled, a contrary part of her wanted to press harder, see if she could really make him laugh.

"I don't agree with everything you say and do. There's a difference. So...now that you know I accept you, appreciate you even, you can go back to bed knowing I'm just like every other woman." She waved toward the hallway.

But he didn't leave. Instead, he reached out and wrapped a red curl around his finger. "Any other woman of my acquaintance would be begging me to kiss her right now."

She snorted to cover her rising panic, because dammit, she wanted to. "Arrogant. How do you know that?"

He smiled, completely unrepentant. "And not one of those women makes me want to pull her up against my body every time she speaks." His voice dropped lower, rasping on her overly sensitized nerves.

"I'm your children's nanny." Her resistance was crumbling in a pathetic heap around her feet, a house built on sand, but she had to try to stop this before it got out of hand. "That's it."

The words echoed inside a strange hollowness that suddenly filled her. Why did knowing all she could ever be to Greyson Masters was a temporary nanny feel like this? Empty. Aching. It made no damn sense. Two weeks and she was smitten. With him and his family. And that was a tragedy worth crying over.

He continued to stare down into her eyes, and desperation had her grasping for a solution—even a shock tactic to stop this, even as she longed for it. With a ragged breath, she curled a hand on his shirt and tugged him closer. "Fine. Just kiss me and get it out of your system, Grey."

Before he could say or do anything, she went up on tiptoe and placed her lips over his.

The kiss caught fire faster than a spark to dead wood.

Grey groaned low in his throat, and aching need took over her body and her mind while he pulled her in close, searing her with the heat of his body. Desire throbbed through every part of her, heavy and thudding, leaving her beautifully tingly and on edge as she lost herself in what he was doing with his lips, his tongue, his hands.

She couldn't have ended it even if she'd wanted to. Gods and goddesses, she'd just discovered what heaven felt like. Taking it away now would be like taking away a child's birthday toy. The sexy stubble on his jaw rasped against her skin, and she reveled in the sensation wanting to press against him, rub her cheek to his. Grey was all man, and she wanted more.

With another groan, he pulled back, then stepped away, breathing hard, and the cool air that hit her in his absence was like being dunked in an ice bath.

He didn't say anything for a long moment. Then he ran his hand through his hair, spiking it up even more than before, making her fingers itch to smooth it down for him. "I shouldn't have done that."

Pride and a fierce self-protective instinct kicked in. She tipped her chin up and gave him her best *nothing big has happened here* smile. Hopefully she managed to look amused and bored at the same time. "You didn't. I did. Now that we got it out of the way, we can move on."

His thick brows slammed low over his eyes, but the kitchen lay in darkness, illuminated only by moonlight and the light on the stairway behind her, so she couldn't catch his expression. "I guess you're right," he said slowly.

He sounded as though he believed her as much as she believed herself. In other words, not at all. But she ignored that, as well as the fire branding her wrist even as the rest of her body cooled. She wasn't even going to sneak a peek at those lines to see if they'd changed. It didn't matter. Whatever those lines meant, and whatever this thing was between her and Grey, it had absolutely no future. Not with who she was and with who he was.

Sometimes the only way to stop a freight train was to blow up the bridge in front of it. "I could never have an affair with an employer. I care about the girls too much."

Grey jerked back as if she'd slapped him. And verbally she just had, because she'd implied that if he continued to pursue her, he didn't care about his kids. An undeniably smart man, he caught her message.

"Of course." The frost in his tone told her everything she needed to know. He'd leave her alone now. "Good night, Rowan."

"Good night, Mr. Masters."

And there went that clenching spasm inside her again as she watched him walk away, each step echoing in the hollow that was her heart.

Damn.

Chapter Nine

"Dad?"

Greyson turned his head to Lachlyn as they all crunched through the snow to the spot from which they teleported. Something in his daughter's voice caught his attention more than normal. "Yes?"

"Some kids at school were talking—"

"Lachlyn," Chloe hissed. "Don't."

Uh-oh.

"I want to know," Lachlyn snapped at Chloe. She turned back to him. "They said our mother was killed by a warlock. Is it true?"

Aw, hell. He had known this conversation would come along someday, but he was hoping for a little more time. Greyson stopped walking. "On the way to school is not a good time to talk about this."

"But—"

He held up a hand, halting Atleigh's protest. "I'll tell you, but tonight when I have time to answer any questions you might have. Okay?"

"So it's true?" The warble in Chloe's voice twisted his gut.

He pulled all three into his arms and kissed the tops of their heads. "Don't worry about it until we talk tonight. Okay?"

He was afraid they'd push it, but all three looked at one another, silently communicating in the way they had, and nodded.

The rest of the morning went as usual as he teleported them to school and returned home. He had eight hours to figure out how much and what to tell his daughters about how their mother had died.

After letting himself into the house, he walked through to the kitchen without really thinking about his direction. There he found Rowan hovering over a pot at the stove. Dressed in jeans and a black sweater, she had the apron he wore when he grilled wrapped around her frame, the material swamping her slim form. Barefooted, she danced and hummed along to the radio, which was tuned to a fifties station.

As he came in, she glanced over her shoulder and smiled like she did each night when he showed up for his cup of tea, though a distance lingered in her eyes that hadn't been there until the colossal mistake of kissing her the other night.

"What are you cooking?" he asked. *I should just go to my office and leave her alone.*

"Sauce for lasagna. My mother's recipe."

"You're not afraid of burning it again?"

She chuckled. "I'm onto your tricks now, mister." She tossed a wink over her shoulder, then turned back to the stovetop, her back to him. "Something bothering you?"

Greyson startled. How had she guessed? Usually people found him hard to read. Leaning a hip against the island counter, he crossed his arms. "What makes you ask?"

She didn't turn around. "You usually go straight into

your office when you get home."

Yup. He should've listened to his instincts. The problem was, his instincts were telling him to ask her for help. He *never* asked for help. "So?"

She lifted a shoulder. "My mother always said I had an intuition for when people needed help. So...?"

Well, hell. Telling her about the girls' middle-of-the-night wanderings had eased a burden for him. Like sharing the weight of the problem. More than he'd expected. Suddenly he wasn't alone in dealing with it, in worrying about it, and, even though the mystery loomed large, he'd felt...lighter... ever since.

Maybe she could do the same for his daughters now? Greyson pulled out one of the stools and plopped down onto it. "This morning the girls asked about how their mother died."

Rowan stopped stirring. "I thought your wife died in childbirth?"

"That's only part of the story, and, apparently, some parents have been talking, because kids at school tipped off the girls."

Rowan was quiet for a long moment, but, with her back to him, he couldn't see her reaction. Finally, she put the spoon down, turned off the burner, and turned to face him. "Kids can be cruel sometimes," she murmured.

"So can adults." He wouldn't mind hunting down the adults who'd helped spread this information. However, the truth had come out broadly among his kind last year. He'd just been waiting for the chain of gossip to reach his family.

"What did you tell them?"

Greyson ran a hand through his hair and blew out a breath. "That I'd talk to them about it tonight. But I have no idea what to say."

To his surprise, Rowan circled the counter and pulled

out the stool beside him. Her hair brushed his cheek as she sat, and her wildflower scent drifted around him. Then she leveled those silvery gray eyes on him. "Tell me first."

Greyson blinked, distracted by her proximity, and had to retrace their conversation. "What will that achieve?"

She gave him a patient look. "Consider it a dress rehearsal. And I can tell you if something would be too much for a twelve-year-old girl to handle."

Something tight in his chest eased a little. Maybe this wouldn't hurt to try.

"Right. Okay." He tapped a finger on the counter, thinking of where to start.

She laid her hand over his, calming his nervous movements with her warmth. He froze, then glanced at her.

"The best place to start is usually at the beginning." She gave his hand a gentle squeeze, then sat back, that wall going right up between them. A brick at a time, but solid.

He tried not to miss the contact, the connection. Instead, he focused on telling her the story.

"My wife and I were both low-level hunters with the Syndicate. In fact, that's how we met. We worked a particularly difficult abuse-of-magic case together, and our supervisor decided we should be partners. We worked together for a year before I got the bright idea of kissing her over dinner one late night."

Greyson smiled at the memory. "I haven't thought of that maybe since Maddie's death."

Rowan gave him a soft smile but said nothing. A good listener. He knew that already from their late-night cups of tea.

"We married a year after that, and she was pregnant a few months later. During that time, we were assigned a case where a warlock was using magic for various illegal ends—theft mostly, some cases of assault, and he was escalating."

Now the hard part.

"What we didn't know was he was tracking *us*. The night Maddie went into labor, he showed up at the house, almost as though he were a Seer and knew the time had come, although, as far as I know, he didn't have that ability."

Greyson could still see every nightmare moment of that night if he closed his eyes. "He chose the right time to strike, with Maddie incapacitated by her pain."

A glance down revealed he'd unconsciously fisted his hands, his knuckles white. With a deep breath, he forced his hands to unclench. "He attacked us in the field as I was teleporting her to the hospital. I defended her, of course, and, eventually, got both of us away. But a stray spell struck her as we fought."

"And she died in childbirth?" she guessed.

Greyson jerked his head in a nod. "Her heart gave out in the end."

Again, Rowan reached across to take his hand. "I'm so sorry, Grey."

Warmth, not the wanting that usually happened when he touched her, but comfort and the sudden sense that he wasn't alone, just like when he'd shared the girls' unknown power with her, flowed from her touch through his skin. He squeezed back in a silent thank-you.

"What happened to the warlock?"

"He disappeared. Officially, they assigned the case to a different hunter. Said I was too emotionally involved."

"He was never found?"

Grey straightened in his seat. "Not for years. But then, last year, he showed up, again using magic to harm others—a nymph and a demigod. The Syndicate gave orders to bring him in."

She must've read the hard satisfaction in his expression, because she let go of his hand, eyes going wide and wary.

"You killed him?"

"I did." He searched her face for any sign of her reaction—revulsion, understanding, anything. But she looked down, hiding her thoughts from him.

After a second, she cleared her throat. "I think you tell the girls that."

Rowan stood and circled the counter, lifting her pot off the stove.

Feeling suddenly untethered, as if he were a balloon she'd released to float away into the sky, Greyson stood. "All of it? You think they're ready?"

"I think they're old enough to understand how she died. I think they also need to know that the man who did it will never hurt them or their family again."

She was right.

He watched her fiddling with the sauce for a long moment but couldn't just walk out. Instead, he moved to stand beside her.

"Thank you."

She flicked a glance his way. "Any time. Now I'd better get this done."

Still oddly reluctant to leave, Greyson forced himself to nod and walk away.

"Grey—"

He turned back at her call.

"I'm...glad you killed him."

Chapter Ten

Greyson sat in the circular room where the Covens Syndicate met weekly and did his best to focus his mind on the discussion. But time and again he found his gaze drawn to the floor-to-ceiling windows and the view beyond.

Situated on the western slopes of the Sierra Nevada, the modern monstrosity the covens had chosen to erect was as different from his woodsy cabin as a demon from an angel. Constructed from cement, steel, and glass, the structure reminded him of an alien spacecraft. However, it did afford incredible views over the tops of the trees and craggy mountaintops to the towering peak of Half Dome in Yosemite in the distance.

At the moment, Alasdair—the most recent head of the Syndicate and Greyson's mentor and friend—droned on about the finances. Each individual coven supported itself independently but also contributed to the Syndicate a tax, which was used for mage-wide business. All business was transacted in gold, of course. While they lived in the wider world, they did their best not to be influenced by it or irrevocably tied to it. Alasdair's report about the gold in their coffers and that in circulation didn't interest Greyson in the least. Not his department, other than the fact that his paycheck drew from that source.

Consequently, he allowed his mind to wander to a redheaded witch whose spunky vulnerability had him thinking things he shouldn't. Freckles and toes and lips that made him...

That damn kiss was stuck in his mind. That and the way sharing things with her seemed to lighten the burden. And, if he was truthful with himself, also what she'd said about the warlock. *I'm glad you killed him.* How had she known he needed to hear that? Needed to know she wasn't appalled by his actions?

And her advice had been spot-on. The girls had cried as he told them about their mother, but knowing their mother's killer would no longer hurt them or anyone else had also visibly relaxed them, comforted them.

He'd tried to thank Rowan before leaving, but she'd waved it off. "You already knew what to say," she said. "You just needed to hear it out loud first."

But she was becoming an obsession, an addiction. As though he needed her close, needed to hear her voice and know what she was thinking. Get her advice. Let her share the burdens. Have her make him smile. He'd forgotten what laughter in his house was like.

She's made it clear. She's just your nanny.

But she was starting to feel like...more. Normally, he'd suspect magical coercion, but the chemistry between them was not remotely forced. Witches had tried to spell him before, compel his affection or even just sex. A subtle difference existed between his body willfully engaging and not—a twitch to his muscles that felt off when not of his own volition. That sensation didn't appear with Rowan. If anything, every part of him strained to be closer even as his logical mind pulled away.

Greyson shifted in his seat as his body responded to his mental image of her, stubborn chin tilted, red curls in wild disarray, gray eyes issuing both warning and appeal. That husky voice calling him Grey. No one had ever shortened his name like that, and he had to admit he liked it on her lips.

His daughters, in their trance, had said her name, said she was connected. To what? To him? To them? To something else? The curiosity might just kill him before he found out. Because if it was to...

Fuck. He was losing it.

Rowan McAuliffe, in a few short weeks, had managed to capture his attention as no other woman ever had. The problem was, she had his attention as a man, but also as a father...and as a witch hunter. None of those aspects seemed compatible with the others.

But too many doubts about her plagued him.

He couldn't ignore her wishes to remain employer and employee only. But what he really couldn't ignore were her powers. Seemingly innocuous. When he'd come up from behind her in the woods, though, she'd ignited energy in her hands without a word uttered, a difficult task for many mages. What really caught his attention, though, was how she'd reabsorbed the energy when he'd revealed his identity. Greyson didn't know a single witch or warlock with that ability. Energy, once directed into a spell, had to be released.

Which begged the question, why was she working as a nanny? A witch with that skill alone would be useful to the Syndicate.

A tap on his tablet brought up her paperwork, which he'd pulled early this morning before teleporting to this meeting. He'd reviewed it, of course, when Delilah had sent over Rowan's info as a potential nanny. Nothing then had caught his attention, and nothing now did, either.

He scanned the facts sheet: Rowan Deirdre McAuliffe. Twenty-seven. Born to a low-level witch and warlock with limited magic who died in a car accident when Rowan was eight. Adopted by a witch named Tanya McAuliffe and raised in Dunbar, on the west coast of Scotland, relatively close to Edinburgh, the coven of which she'd been a member since moving to the area. After a series of unimpressive scores in her witchcraft studies, the Edinburgh Coven determined Rowan to be a witch of minimal skill, and she'd worked a series of relatively low-magic jobs since. The latest being as a nanny.

A perfectly normal background, which had the hunter in him concerned. Given the skill she showed in the forest, her history came across as too bland, off in some way. He just couldn't put a finger on what, exactly. Rowan McAuliffe didn't add up.

"Greyson?"

He lifted his gaze from his phone to find Alasdair staring at him, thick black eyebrows raised in question. Apparently, he'd missed a question directed his way.

Greyson placed his phone facedown on the table. "Sorry. Reviewing some new info. What was the question?"

"We've all read your report. Any updates?"

He didn't need to check the paperwork. "Marius finally found the witch selling illegal potions to humans in New Orleans. She fought back."

"Dead?"

"Yes."

"Well, shit, Greyson. We didn't need yet another example of the Syndicate coming down hard on one of our own."

Alasdair didn't have to point out the warlock Greyson had killed. They were all thinking it. "I know."

That only got a scowl from the man in charge. "Is this

going to be a problem with the Voodoo practitioners down there?"

"Marius has already approached the high priestess. Doesn't look like it."

"Right. Keep us informed. We can't have another incident with them. What else? How is the hunt for the witch involved with that werewolf going?"

Lips tight, Grey leaned forward in his seat. "No progress."

A flash of irritation crossed Alasdair's otherwise passive face. Grey doubted anyone else caught it, but he'd known the man for years.

"What's the holdup?"

"Beyond a physical description—red hair, slender, average height, green or possibly gray eyes—I have nothing else to work with."

"That describes about half the witches in existence." Hestia, Alasdair's sister, who sat to the man's right, leaned forward to speak.

Greyson nodded. "Yes. Approximately five-hundred-thousand witches in the covens meet that description."

"Have the werewolves stated why they didn't take her into custody?" Hestia asked.

"They claim they did and gave her to the demigod Castor Dioskouri, a son of Zeus, apparently. A nymph, Lyleia, now his wife, was Kaios's target in the first place."

Alasdair waved that statement away, as always uninterested in the affairs of any non-mages. "And this Dioskouri, what'd he do with her?"

"He claims he never had her. However, so far, I've had trouble contacting them. They said they'd set up a meeting, but I have yet to hear back." Not a single call returned in weeks now. Why? Were they avoiding him? "On the way home from this meeting, I plan to stop by Dioskouri's offices and try to force the issue."

Alasdair gave a sharp nod. "Good. Employ a truth-teller's spell. I don't like that the wolf shifters allowed her to escape. And with werewolves involved... Given their vengeful natures, they're probably hunting her themselves."

Greyson dipped his head in acknowledgment, even as he gave a mental grimace.

A truth-teller's spell took tremendous amounts of energy. More, he suspected, to apply it to a demigod, if that could be done at all. Alasdair knew this, which meant he knew using the spell would leave Greyson weak and unable to defend himself should things go south.

To risk his best hunter, Alasdair must really want this particular witch.

As the meeting broke up, Greyson gathered his things into his father's old leather attaché case and strode out the double doors. He needed to get outside to teleport. First, though, he needed to make a call.

He fished his phone out of his pocket and searched for a contact.

Delilah.

He hit the button to call and waited for her to pick up.

"This is Delilah."

"Greyson Masters here."

"What can I do for you? How's Rowan?"

Greyson nodded to a few fellow Syndicate members who walked past where he stood just inside the glass doors of the building and waited for them to get farther away. "Actually, I had a few questions about Rowan, if you have a moment."

A short pause greeted his request. "Is she working out okay?"

How did he answer? "So far she's been an excellent nanny. A natural with the girls."

"I'm glad you're pleased," came the smooth rejoinder.

"I am."

"So, what questions do you have?"

"I know you do thorough checks of all employees you staff out."

"Yes."

"Rowan's background indicates she's a witch with minimal powers. However, the other night she was able to manifest energy as a defense."

"She threw energy at you?"

While her tone didn't exactly change, he could picture Delilah, with her catlike dark eyes and long ebony hair no doubt perfectly coifed, sitting forward in her seat. He'd gotten her attention with that, which meant she didn't know.

"She didn't throw them once she realized it was me. I take it by your reaction, you weren't aware of this ability."

"Well, someone should throw some energy at your stubborn head someday." Now lazy amusement laced her voice.

Greyson frowned. Was she avoiding the question?

"Yes, I was aware of this ability," Delilah continued, shutting down his suspicion.

"Then why not list it in the information? For that matter, why is she a nanny with a power like that?"

"Rowan can't control the power. It's a reflex that started when her parents were killed. She was in the car with them, as you know, since you read her bio. A defense mechanism, it rarely manifests. You must've scared her badly. What were you doing?"

Now Greyson didn't want to answer the question.

"I frightened her when we bumped into each other in the middle of the night."

"I see."

Now why did he get the uneasy feeling she knew exactly what they'd been up to that night—not just the girls, but that explosive kiss?

"Well, I hope I've adequately addressed your questions. I'm surprised you didn't just ask her."

Greyson stood up straight, not enjoying the mild rebuke, not to mention the slither of guilt that he'd gone behind Rowan's back with this. "I will next time."

"Good. Though feel free to check with me any time."

"Thanks." After their goodbyes, Grey hung up and slowly tucked his phone back into his pocket. His conversation with Delilah made total logical sense, but something was still itching at him.

Stop being a hunter for a second, and just trust the woman.

First, though, a stop-off in Austin, Texas, to talk to a demigod and a nymph.

Chapter Eleven

Grey killed Kaios's warlock because the guy had murdered his wife.

How she knew for sure that that's who he'd been talking about—the warlock Kaios had used along with Rowan—she didn't know. But it had been plain to her as he'd told the story.

Pain, for Grey, for his wife, for their sweet girls, had oozed through her like Mississippi mud, and Rowan had had to close her eyes against the hard look in his eyes.

But what does that mean for me?

The thought had been swirling around in her head since Grey had told her about it. Plaguing her. Making her question everything she believed. The Syndicate hadn't sanctioned that execution. What if…

Except, Tanya believed they were dangerous. Believed they'd had Rowan's parents killed. Had she been wrong?

A low murmur brought her attention back to where she was, and Rowan observed the girls' lesson with their Aunt Persephone in total silence.

This was the first time she'd come along, because

Greyson had to go into Denver for work on Monday and wouldn't be able to take the girls. Since it was Friday, he'd wanted to introduce her to the girls' aunt, his sister-in-law, ahead of time. Persephone lived "next door," which meant in the Rocky Mountains, but on the other side of the divide. If they drove, the trip would take over an hour.

Hooray for teleporting.

A few glances snuck in Grey's direction—granted, he had his laptop going the entire time—showed he found nothing amiss with the lesson. Was this really how most witches were schooled?

As soon as they had arrived at a cabin not unlike Greyson's with dark brown log siding and natural stone accents, a woman had come out onto her front porch. Rowan pegged her age around thirty, tall and elegant, with dark hair pulled back in a perfect ponytail and wearing three-inch stilettos. In the mountains. In the snow.

Meanwhile, beside her Rowan suddenly felt like a dowdy frump with her red curls a wild halo about her face, and her jeans, black blouse, and black boots way too casual. After the burned lasagna and hiding incident, she hadn't bothered to upgrade her wardrobe all that much, opting for blouses instead of T-shirts. Grey hadn't said anything, but now she questioned her decision. Maybe she'd go shopping again on Sunday when she had her day off.

Only she'd stopped that thinking in its tracks. No way was she changing who she was just to compete with this woman. For what?

The introductions went fine, Persephone asking her to call her by her first name and welcoming her to the area. Then, as the girls tromped inside and they followed, the tone changed subtly. "I do ask that you don't interrupt the lesson." Persephone turned to Greyson. "Remember the last nanny who insisted on helping?" She gave a delicate chuckle.

Grey's eyes narrowed slightly, but he didn't comment.

"I wouldn't dream of interfering," Rowan assured her. Really. She wouldn't. Not having grown up among witches, she hadn't a clue about how they learned their magic.

"Good. Several of your predecessors have been inclined to offer suggestions. I'll tell you what I told them. I've been licensed to instruct for ten years now, and I teach the six- and seven-year-olds at the Denver Coven's gifted academy. I certainly don't need advice from a..." She paused and gave Rowan a cool once-over. "I'm sure you understand."

Amazing how a reasonably worded request could be altered by a tone that spoke volumes. Basically, Persephone had just called her an inept magical user who could never compare to a licensed teacher. Did Grey catch it? A quick check of his expression told her no.

He knew Persephone better than she. Maybe the other woman hadn't meant it that way.

The next few minutes proved that notion wrong. In that short span of conversation, Rowan pegged Persephone as a self-important snob with—if her simpering attitude toward Grey gave any clue—designs on nabbing the widower brother-in-law for herself. Meantime, he, like every other man on the planet, failed to notice the female cattiness happening under his nose, taking the comments at face value.

Rowan schooled her expression to be pleasant. "I'll just observe quietly from the corner. Perhaps I'll even learn something new."

Persephone's smile came across full-on condescending. "Just don't try anything without help."

Wow. The woman *meant* to be a bitch. Persephone's message came across loud and clear: *I'm the better witch* and *hands off.*

"I think she gets the point, Persephone," Grey said in a voice that brooked no argument. "I wouldn't have hired her if I didn't think she was capable."

Okay. So maybe not quite so unobservant. And the warmth that bloomed inside her at his defending her was dangerous.

"It's fine," Rowan said, only to be on the receiving end of his frown.

The other woman paused, then smiled kindly. "I didn't mean anything—"

"I should hope not," Grey said.

Persephone turned to Rowan. "It's nothing against you personally. The other nannies have all had ideas. I'm sure you understand."

Were all traditionally trained witches this competitive? "I can see how frustrating that could be. You have no worries from my side. I promise."

She received a simpering smile for her troubles. "The chair in the corner is comfy." Persephone waved a careless hand.

"Of course," Rowan murmured and moved to the spot on the other side of the room from where Grey had chosen to be.

A childish urge took hold, and she stuck her tongue out at Persephone's back.

A choked sound had her jerking her gaze to Grey, who straightened out the amusement curling his lips and gave her a look that reminded her of Tanya when she was unimpressed.

A sheepish shrug and she'd turned away, wincing as she did. Caught acting like one of the girls when she was supposed to be the adult in charge of them. Just sad. Now, sitting in a literal corner so she wouldn't be "in the way," Rowan couldn't decide which was more difficult—hiding her growing dislike for the woman, hiding her incredulity at the rudimentary lesson taking place given what she'd seen the girls do at home, or hiding her amusement at the girls' obvious boredom with the exercise. Persephone had them growing flowers, but in fast-forward, like watching a time-lapse video—a trick Rowan had learned at the age of five.

"Good job, Atleigh," Persephone praised the now beautifully blooming violets.

Lachlyn rolled her eyes behind her aunt's back. "Aunt Persephone, can we try something else now?"

Persephone ran a critical eye over Lachlyn's single bloom. "Let's focus on getting this spell right first. Once you master the basics, then we'll move on."

It didn't get much more basic than growing a few flowers in a pot.

Rowan bit down on a laugh as Persephone turned her back on Lachlyn to help Chloe, and Lachlyn suddenly showed her true aptitude. With a wave of her hand, the girl grew a bunch of flowers at ten times the speed, resulting in a bouquet similar to her sister's. At Atleigh's warning glance, Lachlyn pulled a face, then reversed time and returned the plant to a single bloom.

Both girls checked the adults in the room—first Persephone and then Grey, who was busy on his laptop. Then they glanced toward Rowan, who raised her eyebrows and again struggled not to laugh out loud at the rueful expressions turned her way. In answer she sent them a conspiratorial wink. Atleigh and Lachlyn blew out silent breaths of relief even as they exchanged a glance. Persephone chose that moment to turn back to them, and Rowan remained quiet in her assigned corner.

After all, Persephone had been quite clear about not wanting any help.

Twenty minutes later, torture in the guise of a lesson finally over, the group made their way out of the house. "Great job, ladies," Persephone praised her nieces. "Lachlyn, I expect you to be able to bloom more flowers by the time I see you on Monday."

"Yes, ma'am," the girl grumbled.

Persephone turned to Rowan. "Lovely to meet you. I hope you last longer than the others."

Sure you do.

Before Rowan could respond in a suitably nanny-like manner, a hummingbird appeared and hovered before her, staring right at her.

"Look at that," Grey commented. "I've never seen a hummingbird do that."

"Oh." Rowan gave a self-conscious giggle, which sounded forced to her ears. "It must think all this red hair is a really big flower."

Of course, that wasn't what the hummingbird thought at all.

Danger, the tiny bird whispered, and Rowan clenched her fists against a spasm of fear. Pricklies hit in a shiver-inducing wave spiking through her skin, and she had to physically keep herself from glancing into the surrounding woods for someone secretly watching.

The wolves aren't coming for you. Greyson is the bigger problem.

Collecting her calm like pulling a cloak around her, Rowan focused. She was the only one here who could understand the small bird, unless any of the others were Anevals—witches whose magic was strongest in connection to animals. She couldn't talk to the bird, though. Not here.

Being an Aneval was more power than a barely magical user like she was pretending to be should have. Worse, if the Syndicate found out the weakness inherent with the power, it would be just one more nail in her coffin as far as they were concerned.

"Aren't you beautiful. But no nectar here. Come back later and I'll have some flowers for you." She held her breath, hoping the creature understood.

Danger is coming, it whispered before zipping away with a high-pitched hum of its beating wings.

Spider eyes and ghost tears. Maybe she should've been listening to those pricklies all along?

"Do animals often come to you?" Grey asked, his dark brown gaze assessing.

Rowan hitched a shoulder. "I guess."

Relief whooshed through her as the small frown between his eyebrows eased. "You must have a touch of Aneval in you."

"I'm sure it's just a coincidence," Rowan hurried to say.

"Such a rare and valued gift," Persephone murmured. "I'm sure Rowan's right. Coincidence."

But Grey wasn't dropping it. "Do they ever talk to you?"

How to answer without directly lying? Ironically, Persephone's disdain for the possibility of a nanny possessing such a skill gave her the answer. "If they did, I probably would be doing something else." She took the sting out of the response with a cheerful smile.

At that he laughed, and Rowan sucked in a sharp breath. Normally Grey's expression tended toward stern, unmovable. But when he smiled, like now, he showed an entirely different side—boyish, fun-loving. She had the strangest urge to laugh with him.

"Let's go," Grey said.

After a parting kiss on his cheek from Persephone, the five of them stood in a circle in front of her house, hands clasped tightly. "Home."

Just the one word from Grey and they disappeared. Rowan had heard of others getting violently ill from the trip. Still others indicated teleportation to be a frightening practice. But she'd always loved the sensation. Instead of nausea or terror, Rowan found the experience fascinating.

They didn't appear to be moving. Rather, the five of them

stayed still while the world whooshed by in a silent blur of colors. Here in the mountains, shades of greens and browns and grays, the white of the snow with the blue of the skies overhead streaked with white from the clouds, surrounded her.

In moments they arrived in the front yard of Greyson's home. The trees and brown winter grass around them flattened for a moment beneath the gust of wind generated by their arrival. Rowan released her grip on Chloe and Lachlyn and turned to head inside.

"Have you teleported often?" Grey asked.

"Um—" She hesitated to answer. How rare was teleportation anyway? Did most witches do it a lot? "Not often," she hazarded. "But I do enjoy it."

Interest lingered in his dark eyes as he walked beside her. "Oh? Most find it disconcerting. What do you enjoy?"

Had that been the wrong answer? Too late to change it now. "It's like the universe comes to you, and I love all the colors. I imagine setting up a room of Monet paintings and then spinning in circles might have the same effect."

"I've never heard that description, but I do see what you mean."

"Do you like it?" Curiosity always had been a weakness of hers. Grey was quickly becoming another weakness.

As he unlocked the door, he flicked her a glance she couldn't interpret. "I do."

He let them inside, then promptly disappeared into his office. She frowned after his departing form. What had she said wrong this time?

It doesn't matter. Distance is what you wanted.

She gave herself a shake. As long as he believed her story, his feelings about her, one way or another, should make no difference. The more important question at this moment was how she was going to find time to get away today. She needed to talk to the hummingbird.

Normally, she'd take her Sunday to disappear for a bit, but this weekend, the triplets were staying home for once. Grey had already asked her to stick around, saying he'd give her both Saturday and Sunday off the following weekend. She couldn't wait that long.

Danger is coming, the hummingbird had said. Had the witches discovered her, and Grey played it cool? Or did a different danger lurk in the woods?

Chapter Twelve

Rowan wasn't quite sure what to do with herself the rest of the day. On Saturdays they took the girls out. And Sundays she occupied herself while Grey took to the girls to visit one or the other of their grandparents.

But today was different. Hanging out in the house with the girls around but nothing for them to do was weird. Now they were up in their rooms, leaving her alone with Grey, who, for once, came out of his office. They sat at opposite ends of the family room—him binge-watching a favorite show on TV and her reading a book with Nefertiti curled up in the crook of her bent legs, snoring softly.

Only she'd read the same damn paragraph over and over for about twenty minutes now. Rowan hid a sigh and hopped up.

"Tea?" she asked.

Grey's ready smile set her heart fluttering like a hummingbird's wings. He'd been doing that more lately. "It's not nighttime," he teased.

"We'll do a black tea then and risk the caffeine."

"You and your tea." He shook his head.

"Is that a no?"

"Actually, it sounds good."

Almost on autopilot, Rowan moved to the stovetop where she got out the teapot, filling it with water.

Grey appeared at her side and, without a word and in perfect tandem, he got out the teacups and the tin of loose-leaf tea. She reached in a drawer to hand him the infusers, which he filled.

Before she knew it, they were leaning against the counter, sipping warm, soothing liquid like they did every night. Some nights they talked for hours, others they sat together in companionable quiet. Like now. But right now, in the middle of the day when it was harder to pretend they were living in a different world, it struck her how…homey…a picture they made. A pleasant habit. Almost as though they'd been doing this for years. Rowan closed her eyes, but couldn't remove the images of what they could be if…

If nothing.

A series of sharp pings sounded and Grey pulled out his cell phone to check the screen. "What the hell?"

Rowan peeked over the top of her cup to find Grey staring at his phone.

Uh-oh. Slowly, she buried her face in the tea. Was he only just now figuring out his phone had an issue? It had been weeks since she'd cast that spell. No way was she that good. He had to have noticed the issue sooner, right?

Another hiss of frustration followed by mutterings. "No wonder."

"What?"

"I knew there was something wrong with my phone. I thought I'd missed a few calls. People have said they left messages, which I didn't get. Well, I guess they all just showed up at once, thirty missed messages."

A quick peek revealed his disgruntled expression as, one after the other, he listened to each voice mail. Laughter burbled up from a wicked place inside her. She couldn't stop the small snigger that escaped.

"Did you say something?"

Rats. With effort she composed her expression into something she hoped was suitably innocent. "Did you leave it on silent accidentally?" Not laughing at his offended expression ended up being harder than she'd thought, or she might've kept her mouth shut.

"No," he snapped.

With a shrug she raised her book again.

"Rowan?" Chloe's voice preceded her into the room as she tromped down the wooden stairs with all the finesse of a twelve-year-old girl.

"In here," Rowan called. She set her cup down on the counter.

Chloe appeared in the doorway. "Can I ask you something?"

"What do you need, Chloe?" Grey asked.

Rowan had to give the man props. His question wasn't brusque or condescending. He truly wanted to help.

"Um. This is something I need Rowan's help with. Thanks, Dad."

"Okay." He said the word slowly, but let it go.

The glance he flicked her way held an emotion she couldn't quite identify. Trust, if she didn't know better. Delilah had warned her about Grey's questions lately. Trust wasn't something she'd earned with him yet.

Shaking off the worry, and curious anyway, Rowan followed when Chloe beckoned her into the foyer.

"What's up?"

Chloe checked behind Rowan first. "I started my period," she whispered, cheeks turning red.

Oh. "Oh." Rowan mentally winced at her lame response. Time to rally. "Well, welcome to womanhood, sweetie. You'll find out quickly enough that periods are a pain in the rear, but it's exciting to start. Now…when I started, I was horribly embarrassed. But my friend Maureen was thrilled. Which one are you?"

Chloe wrinkled her nose. "Embarrassed."

"Got it. In that case, I'll save the banner and cake, and no announcements at dinner." Rowan winked, and Chloe relaxed enough to giggle.

A small glow of pride and happiness sparked in her heart. She'd been helpful in a big moment in Chloe's life. Suddenly, that glow snuffed out, to be replaced by a bleak thought. She was going to miss this family when the time came to leave. She hadn't expected to connect with them in such a short span, but she loved Atleigh's need to be the peacemaker, and Chloe's shy side, and Lachlyn's sass.

And Grey who made her feel…

Nothing. Because she couldn't let herself.

Giving a mental shake of her head, she focused on Chloe. "Okay. Have either of your sisters started?"

Chloe shook her head.

"You don't have products? Tampons? Pads?"

If anything, the poor girl's cheeks reddened further, the color climbing down her neck and over her chest. "No."

Rowan held up her hand. "No problem. We'll just go to the grocery store in town and get some."

"Do I have to go, too?" Mortification laced every syllable.

Rowan considered their options. "How about this… we'll go together, because I want to point out some different options and let you choose. Then you can go wait in the car while I pay for them. Sound good?"

Chloe considered that for a moment. "Okay."

"I'll go grab my purse. Tell your dad you're helping me

get stuff for dinner and meet me at the truck. Right?"

To her shock Chloe flung her skinny arms around her neck and squeezed tightly. "Thanks, Rowan. I knew you'd help."

And there goes my heart.

After grabbing her purse, Rowan popped her head into the family room. "I'm running to the grocery store for some stuff for dinner. Chloe's going to come with me. Lachlyn and Atleigh are upstairs."

He looked up from his phone, apparently still fiddling with the thing. "Do I want to know?"

She glanced over her shoulder, sensitive to Chloe's feelings. "Chloe started her period," she whispered.

Grey dropped his phone. "Oh."

The total panic in his eyes pulled a grin from her. "No big deal. I've got this."

Rather than pressing her for details or demanding to be in the know, Grey nodded. "I'm sure you can handle it."

"You okay?"

He cleared his throat as he picked up the phone. "I'll let you know when I get over the shock."

Rowan chuckled, even as guilt pricked at her. How was she going to leave them? Betray them? One more person to disappoint them. "It's under control."

Keys jangling, she hustled out of the house before she did something stupid like confess everything. Something about this man demanded total trust. A seductive idea, and one she couldn't give in to. Ever.

Chapter Thirteen

After hours of dealing with returning calls and catching up on everything his phone had missed and dumped on him in one shot, Greyson hung up the phone and swore under his breath. When he'd dropped by Castor Dioskouri's office last week, he'd expected to set a meeting date for that week, but they'd claimed to be too busy with work. You'd think the plane manufacturing industry wouldn't be quite so urgent, but apparently not. Consequently, they'd set the meeting date for today—over a week later.

Only Lyleia, or Leia as she'd asked him to call her, had just called to say Tala and Marrok Canis-Banes, the wolf shifter alphas joining them, couldn't make it to the Syndicate's Denver office. Something to do with another meeting with other wolf shifter alphas going too long. No way was he letting them reschedule again. He'd lost so much time that the trail was growing colder and colder with each day that passed. This was his one and only lead.

"Where are the alphas meeting?" he asked Leia.

"At the Canis-Banes camp, on the eastern side of Rocky

Mountain National Park."

"That works out. I happen to live nearby. If you and Castor don't mind driving up from Denver, why don't we all meet at my house after they've finished their meeting?"

"Oh…we couldn't put you out."

Greyson glared at the wall. They were definitely avoiding him. He had yet to figure out how they'd manipulated his phone, but that had to be the only explanation for the darn thing not working. "No bother at all. In fact, I'd say you could stay here, but it's a smaller house, one of the original structures built before the park boundaries were even established. I'll put you up at the Stanley. It's a gorgeous hotel. I think you'll enjoy it."

"We've stayed there before." A smile came through in her voice. "Let me check with the others, but that sounds lovely."

They set a time and, before they hung up the phone, Leia promised to contact him only if a problem arose.

"Rowan!" Greyson grimaced at the frustration he'd allowed to leak into his voice. As he strode through the house in search of his nanny, he tempered the emotion. "Row—"

"I heard you the first time you bellowed."

He spun around in the kitchen to find her standing in the doorway that led down to her basement rooms.

And promptly lost all thought of what he was going to say, the words swirling down a drain along with shock.

Rowan's glorious red hair had changed color—turned raven-wing black with a streak of purple through the bangs. Straight as a broomstick, it hung in a glossy curtain to her waist. Meanwhile, her skin had turned an interesting shade of light pink. Her eyes had changed color as well—one emerald green, and one an eerie turquoise.

And suddenly he was struggling with an almost savage need to turn her back. This colorful creature wasn't *his* Rowan.

The ridiculousness of that thought had his words coming out more harshly than intended. "What in the seven hells happened to you?"

She plopped her hands on her hips, her pointed little chin tipping up as she stared him down. "I was practicing some of the magic the girls are learning."

That stubborn chin got added to the growing list of things he wanted to kiss—freckles, lips, chin, and yes, even those cute toes. She'd probably smack him in the head, or worse, if he laughed, but, damn, she made it hard not to sometimes. "So this is…on purpose?"

She lifted a single eyebrow, daring even one snigger or word of criticism to escape his lips. "What do you think?"

Greyson recognized dangerous ground, feeling the metaphorical quicksand sinking away under his feet. He couldn't offer help and risk offending her, but what if she needed it?

When he didn't answer, she sighed. "What did you want?"

Still distracted by her bizarre appearance, it took him a moment to answer. "Instead of going to Denver for my meeting, they are going to come to the house tonight around five."

She leaned a hip against the island counter. "Okay. I'll be at Persephone's with the girls, as we already arranged, when they arrive. Do you need me to feed everyone?"

"That would be good. As well as having appetizers and drinks ready."

She nodded.

"How many?"

"Four."

"Mages? Or something else?"

Now why would she ask that? "Why?"

"In case they have any special dietary needs or preferences. I'd like to plan ahead if I can."

Suspicion drained out of him. Gods, he needed to start trusting more. Especially Rowan. "I see. A demigod, a nymph, and two wolf shifters."

She raised her eyebrows. "That's quite a crowd. Sounds like the beginning of a bad joke."

"Have you dealt with their kind before? You don't have to be nervous."

"Oh... Good." She turned away to open the pantry. "I don't think that means anything different, but I'll look it up, just in case. Maybe red meat for the wolves would be appropriate. Or fish for the nymph? Or maybe she'd be offended by that." She was muttering more to herself than talking to him. Now she glanced over her shoulder. "Are nymphs friends with fish? Or do they eat them?"

He had to bite back a laugh, something that happened more and more around her. "I have no idea."

"You're no help then. I'll look it up," she repeated. "Anything else? Where are they staying?"

"I'm putting them up at the Stanley Hotel in Estes Park."

"So no need to move the girls around," she commented.

"No."

"What time should I plan to serve dinner? It's probably best if I prep ahead of time before taking the girls to their lesson at five."

Right. How long would it take him to get all the details and discern the truth? "Let's eat around seven. That should be plenty of time to wrap up our meeting."

"Sounds good." With a cheerful smile that appeared almost sinister given her one turquoise eye, she pulled open the fridge door, ostensibly to figure out her meal plan. "What's the meeting about?"

Suspicion again crept up on him, tugging at his gut. "It's Syndicate business."

Her shoulders stiffened, but she didn't turn around. "I

see."

Damn. Now he'd offended her. "Sorry—"

She turned, holding up one hand, strange eyes wide and innocent. "I understand. Your work is very secretive. No need to explain."

With that, she turned back to the fridge. "Now, if you don't mind, I'd better take stock and then go back into town for groceries."

Effectively dismissed—a sensation Greyson never encountered, especially with women—he found himself reluctant to leave. "Can I help?"

She didn't even bother to turn around, keeping her head in the fridge. "No, thanks."

Rather than push it, he headed back to his office, pausing in the doorway. "You will look…like yourself when they arrive?"

She snorted as she poked her head around the fridge door. "We'll see, but I'll make myself scarce anyway. As the nanny, it seems more appropriate. I'll eat downstairs."

Like hell. Greyson refused to examine too closely why her assumption sent a sharp wave of knee-jerk protest through him, but everything in him rejected the image of Rowan playing the servant. "No. You'll eat with us."

Her mouth tightened, and he waited for the argument. But it didn't come. "Fine."

Chapter Fourteen

At five o'clock, a demigod, nymph, and two alpha wolf shifters sat down on the couch and chairs in Greyson's family room, without a single excuse or call telling him they wouldn't come. All day he'd been waiting for his phone to ring. But instead, here they sat.

Leia was a petite honey-blonde with sapphire-blue eyes. Nymphs were known for their beauty, and she proved to be no exception. Beside her on the couch sat Castor, looking exactly how Greyson would've expected a demigod to appear—suave, arrogant, and just missing pretty thanks to the muscles.

Quite familiar with wolf shifters, as they pervaded these mountains, Tala and Marrok Canis-Banes were prime examples of those paranormal creatures, both tall with inherent grace and power behind every move. Marrok was dark, gray streaking his temples, where Tala was a pale blonde.

As a warlock, attuned to the energy around him, the air practically crackled with the power the foursome before him brought into the house, standing the hairs on the back of his neck on end.

Greyson leaned forward, elbows propped on his knees. "I'm familiar with the whos, whats, and whys. However, I'd like to hear directly from you what went down the day a witch was used by the werewolf Kaios against you."

Tala, Marrok, and Castor all looked to Leia, who made a face. "I'm afraid this story starts over a millennium ago."

Quickly, she detailed how she'd humiliated the werewolf, Kaios, and his vendetta against her. How he'd caught up with her at Tala and Marrok's wedding, and she'd gone against him again when she'd helped the alphas fake a sign from the gods, implying their mating of convenience was blessed. Kaios hadn't taken that well and attacked first the nymphs, using the warlock Greyson had later killed. Then he'd come for her where she'd set a trap, hidden in a cabin in the woods. That's where they'd come across Kaios's witch.

"During the ensuing fight, Castor knocked her out, restoring powers to those she'd turned off," Leia wrapped up.

"If she was unconscious, how did she get away?" This was the crux of the entire issue.

The four exchanged a glance before Marrok spoke up. "After everything was over, I'm afraid we were all busy with different things. I'm not sure who had the witch or who didn't. Or how she got away."

Greyson allowed silence to fall over the room as he took in their words. With a release of breath, he ran his hand over his jaw, his evening stubble scratching at his palms. Not that he wasn't convinced, but he needed to be sure. "The Syndicate wanted me to use a truth spell on you."

All four stiffened. "But you didn't?" Castor asked.

Greyson dropped his hand. "No. But, with your permission, I'd like to cast a spell to review your memories of the event."

A window behind him slammed open as a gust of wind assailed the house. For the smallest of moments, Greyson would've sworn a woman shouted, "No." A cold chill skittered up his neck, similar to the one he often experienced near the fireplace. However, as he jumped up to close the window, none of the others commented.

"Sorry," he apologized as he resumed his seat.

The wind could be rough up here. It was nothing to worry about, and there happened to be more important things on which to focus. "Old house. Anyway... Not that I don't trust you, but seeing your memories will allow me to corroborate your stories. Plus, I might be able to see through your eyes what happened to her, accessing a memory you can't."

Another exchange of glances before Leia straightened in her seat. "You can start with me."

"Thank you." Most powerful creatures in the world would never allow such an invasion.

Grey moved to sit on the coffee table in front of her and took her hands. "I want you to think of that day, picture it in your mind."

"Okay."

"Can you see it?"

"Yes."

The lights flickered as he whispered his spell, and a tug pulled through his body as his energy depleted in order to feed the complicated cast he attempted.

Closing his eyes, immediately he was transported inside the memory, seeing a new scene as if he were Leia— experiencing every sense as she did, every emotion, every nuance, exactly how she'd lived it. She and Castor stood in a flat field, facing the ancient werewolf, Kaios.

Behind him, out of the darkness, a line of wolf shifters, already shifted into their animal form, advanced upon them. Castor stepped closer and took her hand, presenting a united front. Above them, the skies darkened with the warning of the demigod's wrath, swirling with dark clouds.

"Oh, I have a way to deal with you." Kaios turned to signal someone over his shoulder. A woman with deep red hair stepped out of her hiding spot. She raised her arms and whispered words Leia couldn't catch. The clouds cleared in an instant, returning to the blue skies of moments before.

Castor's hand twitched in Leia's.

The woman closed her eyes, her face a study of regret. Leia got the impression the woman would rather be anywhere than here right now.

"I'm sorry," the woman mouthed at her, misery pinching her face.

The woods were eerily quiet—no bird chirped, no animals scurried through the underbrush. They'd all gone into hiding.

Done with the memories involving the witch, as far as Leia knew, Greyson watched as Leia killed Kaios. Frustration shot through him as, fighting ended, she returned to the cabin with no trace of the witch to be seen.

Releasing her hands, Greyson opened his eyes to find the others watching in silent curiosity. "Right. Marrok, you're next."

Castor's perspective would be too much like Leia's. He'd still check it, but first he wanted a different viewpoint.

Repeating the steps he had taken with Leia, an even stronger surge of energy was required to access the alpha werewolf's memories. Spelling a person who possessed powers or abilities always took more.

Marrok's memories of the same scene started from within the trees. Kaios's appearance and the start of the fight up until Castor disappeared with Leia were similar. Again, the witch's contrition and reluctance appeared genuine and obvious.

Experiencing the memory from Marrok's perspective,

the shifter's heightened sense of smell caught the trace of the witch's scent, and Greyson jerked. The light floral wildflowers and honey reminded him of someone.

Rowan.

But it couldn't be.

Shock clawed at him as he took a closer look at the witch standing miserably behind Kaios. No. He would've recognized her sooner. The witch in their memories held some similarities, the same dark red, curling hair, similar height and build. But her face appeared nothing like Rowan, and her eyes were green instead of gray.

Relief surged through him, and he continued watching from Marrok's point of view.

After he and Tala dealt with a few of the rogue wolf shifters helping Kaios, Marrok searched the trees for the redheaded witch who'd been holding Castor's powers at bay. Had she done the same to the nymphs? If so, what stopped her now?

Sure enough, Castor stood over the witch's limp form. Lightning sprang from the demigod's fingertips, blinding in brilliance, crackling with power, the scent of burned ozone rancid in his nose, overpowering the earthy scents of wolf shifters and underlying metal of blood. The electricity in the air had Marrok's fur standing on end. With a boom of thunder, Castor fried the wolf closest to him, but he left the witch unharmed, beyond knocking her unconscious. Good. Marrok's impression was the woman had been forced to use her magic against them.

No other memories of the witch.

Greyson released Marrok's memories and turned to his mate. The energy required to access Tala's memories surprised him, as the amount was greater than what he'd needed for her mate, which was interesting, but irrelevant to his purposes. Tala's memories confirmed Marrok's. Finally, he turned to Castor. By the time he finished with the demigod, Greyson's entire body shook from the effort. He clenched his fists at the sensation, trying to keep the spots dancing behind his eyes at bay.

And his frustration had only grown. At least now he knew what the witch looked like. However, none of the four had seen what happened to her after Kaios's death. They'd been telling him the truth, as now he'd seen with his own eyes—through their perspective, but still confirmation.

Damn. Now what?

He'd hoped some clue might present itself, giving him a next step in his hunt. But no fucking luck.

"Are you protecting her?" He couldn't ignore the evidence that pointed to the obvious.

"Yes." Leia said. No hesitation.

"Why? She helped attack you. Because of her, Kaios could've killed you."

"She didn't want to help him. He was making her. Even you could see that."

Greyson couldn't deny the truth of the statement, not now that he'd experienced the scene for himself through their memories. All four of them had come to the same conclusion.

"Why not turn her over to us, though?"

Leia gave him a direct stare. "She's terrified of the Covens Syndicate. Afraid they'll execute her first and ask questions later. Like you did with the warlock who attacked my sisters."

Chapter Fifteen

Death warmed over probably felt better than Rowan did at that moment. She'd just spent the last hour doing everything she could to alter the memories Greyson walked through to make sure he wouldn't recognize her.

Delilah had assured her the four powerful individuals now in the house had sworn to protect her secrets. Still, Rowan had done what she could to disguise her appearance. Damn good thing she'd magically bugged Greyson's office. As soon as she'd heard him invite Leia and the others to the house, she'd done a number on her hair, skin, and eyes.

Grey's face when he'd seen her had been the only pleasant moment in an otherwise shitty day.

The magic to change her appearance had barely taxed her energy, but that was nothing compared to what she'd just put her body through.

After their lessons with Persephone, she'd brought the girls home as planned, arriving by the transportation key Grey had provided to convey her and the girls to and from Persephone's. Not wanting to be seen, Rowan had cautiously let Chloe, Atleigh, and Lachlyn into the house, holding a finger to her lips to indicate the need to remain quiet.

She'd listened for a long moment and concluded Grey's meeting wasn't yet over, and he was in the family room. So she turned to the girls, waving her hand in a shooing motion. "Your dad's not done yet. Go on upstairs and work on your homework until I call you down for dinner."

With long faces the three turned to the stairs. "Will we at least get to see the demigod?" Chloe grumbled.

Ah. That explained why they'd been eager to hurry home. Rowan narrowed her eyes. "They're staying for dinner, so yes. You'll meet all of your father's guests."

Smiles of glee followed the sound of elephants stamping up the old wooden stairs. Nothing like subtle signs they were home. She waited for Grey to check, but he didn't come out.

If they were still in a meeting, maybe she could listen in? Do more to help cover her tracks?

With not an ounce of remorse, she quietly let herself back outside. She didn't need to be caught performing such a complicated spell. One Tanya had taught her. One that took both effort and skill. One which, if she were to hold it too long, could become permanent. But Tanya had said that happened after five days, so Rowan figured ten or twenty minutes would be fine.

Drawing on the energy generated by the natural world— the friction of the wind over the earth, the dissipating warmth of the sun, the solid presence of the mountains under her feet—she whispered her demonic words.

Peta babkama luruba ma ina etuti asbu kima bu'idu.

Open the gate for me that I may enter here and dwell in darkness as a wraith.

A ghost, but one tied to a still-living body.

Cold seeped into her skin, then deeper into her gut, and finally into her very bones. As her body passed into the netherworld where spirits lingered, her soul shuddered, clinging to her humanity, her memories. Finally, the world turned to muted shades, as though a sheer curtain had been drawn over her eyes.

Her first few steps felt as though lead boots had been strapped to her feet, but as she moved, the sensation lessened. Slowly, she glided through the door and into the house, down the hall, and to the family room where Grey sat with four people she might never be able to forget.

Even in her half-dead spectral form, with her emotions muted much like her sight, the regret that lingered every day over her part in Kaios's evil throbbed through her. If the Covens Syndicate ever found out werewolves and other types of shifters could control an Aneval...Rowan shuddered at the thought, fear reaching her even here.

The more powerful the creature, the more control they had over a witch whose main gift involved speaking to animals—something about the connection involved. All she knew was Kaios, an ancient and extremely powerful werewolf, had only to whisper a command and her body would follow while her mind remained horribly disconnected, unable to control her actions in any way.

Even if they hadn't sanctioned some of the executions Rowan knew of, including the warlock Grey killed, the Syndicate would have her put down like a rabid beast when they found out about this. Maybe they should. Maybe she was defective.

But then, they might go after *every* Aneval. The threat posed by such a weakness would surely be deemed too great to risk. If they didn't kill Anevals, they'd imprison them—to keep them safe, of course, but the result would be the same regardless of the intentions.

Wouldn't they?

Grey was making her question her assumptions more and

more. Not enough to let him find out about her yet, though.

Grey broke the silence she'd walked in on. "The Syndicate wanted me to use a truth spell on you."

All four people in the room stiffened. "But you didn't?" Castor asked.

Greyson dropped his hand. "No. But, with your permission, I'd like to cast a spell to review your memories of the event."

"NO!" Rowan shouted. Surprise and gut-wrenching fear punching the denial from her.

A window behind Grey slammed open as a gust of wind assailed the house. She wasn't sure who was more shocked by that window bursting open, her or Grey. Then, again, she knew what had caused it, and he didn't. Unfortunately, the small interruption didn't stop him from accessing their memories.

One by one, Leia, Marrok, Castor, and Tala each submitted to having Grey in their heads. They each tried to keep from showing her so he wouldn't recognize her. However, Greyson Masters was one of the most powerful mages she'd encountered and had moved past their blocks and attempts with ease, seeing exactly what he needed to see.

Rowan, panicked and unable to think of a better way, drew on every single ounce of energy available to her in the spirit realm—an unusual amount. His house must be a portal for many dead. She even drew from the four powerful people before her as much as she could, separated from them by the veil of death.

In each memory involving her, she changed the shape of her face, the shade of her eyes. She couldn't do much more and only prayed her actions had been enough. Finally, Grey had finished. With the last miniscule bit of energy she possessed, Rowan drifted outside and pushed herself back into the world of the living, a sensation akin to rubbing sandpaper over her skin.

A close thing. Getting out of the spirit realm after draining herself altering those memories in real time had been like moving through hot tar, leaving her so exhausted she almost didn't have enough fight in her to do it.

But she made it out.

Mental note to only use that trick to observe next time. No magic within magic.

Then, with stumbling, plodding steps, she'd snuck around the house to the basement entrance.

Now the reflection staring back at her in the bathroom mirror with her mismatched eyes showed a woman with skin a sickly shade of gray, lips pinched and pale, and a dew of perspiration across her brow. For the second time in as many minutes, her stomach heaved, and she pitched over the toilet. Not that she had anything left to empty.

Dry heaving sucked more than vomiting.

A soft touch pressed up against her, and she lifted her head to find Nefti there to comfort. Only, as often happened around the cat, that strange shivery cold passed through her. Almost like an impetus to get her ass moving.

Right. She needed to finish getting dinner ready for Greyson's guests—four people who could give her away with a simple wrong comment or look.

Forcing herself to move, she leaned over the sink, splashing cool water on her skin. What she really needed right now was sugar. Lots of it. She gave her pitiful reflection a grimace. She'd fix it, but, unfortunately, if she used more magic, she'd pass out. Nothing she could do now. As things stood, she was barely standing anyway.

"Rowan?" Grey's voice drifted down the stairs. "Are you down there?"

She cracked the door. "Yes," she croaked. Then she cleared her throat, took a deep breath, and tried again. "Yes."

"I thought I heard you come in with the girls. Our meeting is over."

"I'll be right up," she called back.

How am I going to show my face? Grey will know something's horribly wrong. Granted, he wasn't feeling too hot himself. Performing that memory spell on one creature as powerful as a demigod had to be taxing. On four powerful persons should've knocked him on his ass. She should know; she'd just done something similar.

A snuffling sound at her back door had her whirling to see the shadow of a massive figure outside. Now what?

Witch? The low rumbling word came from the creature on the other side. An animal had come to her in a human dwelling?

Slowly and haltingly, she stumbled to the door. Opening it, she gasped to find a massive grizzly bear standing on the tiny patio, shaded by the porch above, close enough to smell his hot breath, feel the warmth of his massive body. It was oddly tempting to snuggle into his thick brown fur, despite the trepidation pumping her sluggish blood through her at a slightly faster rate. Would he feel soft or coarse against her skin?

You need help, the bear said.

How did you know?

We can sense you. You need help.

Did the bear even know what he offered? Rowan bit her lip. She'd never drawn energy from an animal before, but a creature as massive as this, filled with raw natural power... Could he help?

Reaching out a hand, she placed it against his shoulder. *Soft. He's so soft.*

Through sheer force of will, she drew the energy from him, from his life force. She had to be careful not to draw so much she left him vulnerable, just enough, thank the fates, to help her. Her body remained exhausted, but at least she was functioning.

Reluctant to break the connection, she slowly drew her hand back. "Thank you."

Danger comes this way. You should run.

Fear again spiked inside her, the taste of it acrid in her mouth, although that might be the vomit from earlier. "What danger?"

I don't know. I've heard only whispers.

"Who would know?"

The birds who can fly highest.

A falcon or an eagle perhaps. She had to find out after this was over. She couldn't stay safe if she didn't know what she had to protect herself from. "Again, I thank you."

The bear bowed his giant head, then turned and lumbered away, blending into the night, a large shadow climbing the hill and finally disappearing into the trees.

"Rowan?" Grey's voice again drifted down the stairs.

Thankfully, he hadn't come down to find out what the holdup was. Quickly, she shut her back door. "Coming!"

Getting up the stairs when her legs resembled limp noodles more than bone and blood took concentrated effort, but she made it. And entered a full kitchen.

"Here she is," Grey said, as he stepped to her side. "I'd like to introduce you to the woman who keeps my home running like clockwork. This is Rowan McAuliffe."

As he raised a shaking hand to her back, she gave him a closer look. Wrecked. The man was wrecked. "You need sugar."

Rather than respond, he tipped his head toward his guests.

Taking the hint, she turned to them, smile fixed. "Lovely to meet you."

She received smiles in return, though confused ones,

and caught Castor's questioning glance, taking in Rowan's appearance, and the way Leia dug her elbow into his side.

Which reminded her. Rowan put a self-conscious hand to her hair. "Sorry about the strange look. Normally I'm a redhead, but magic practice went a bit...awry." She rolled her eyes for effect.

"The pink skin is surprisingly lovely," Tala said. "But the eyes are a bit..."

"Off-putting?" Rowan grinned. "Sorry about that. Hopefully, it doesn't ruin your dinner."

"Not at all," Leia said, with a pointed look at Castor and Marrok. The wolf shifter smiled kindly, saying nothing, while the demigod sent his wife a frown, earning him a shake of her head.

"I'll call the girls down," Grey said.

Rowan still didn't like the pallor in his face. "I'll call them." But first she went to the drawer that held the candy and pulled out two chocolate bars.

One she stuffed in her pocket, the other she shoved in his hands. "Eat it."

Then she headed upstairs to get the girls, stuffing her face with the other chocolate bar. The girls eagerly abandoned their homework and followed her down the stairs. She walked into the kitchen, where she was happy to note Grey's returning color.

"By the gods!"

At Castor's exclamation, every person in the room turned to face him.

"Cas?" Leia asked.

The demigod's blue eyes blazed with a terrifying light as he rounded on Greyson. "You didn't tell me your daughters were fates."

Chapter Sixteen

"What the hell are you talking about?" Greyson demanded.

The chocolate Rowan had practically force-fed him had eased his shaking, but he wasn't anywhere near full strength yet. Would he need it to face down a demigod? Given the heavy glare Castor was directing at his daughters, fear speared icy fingers through Greyson's heart, along with a shot of adrenaline spiking his blood.

He couldn't lose them, too.

Greyson moved to put himself bodily between the threat and his children.

"Cas, darling," Leia placed a steady hand on the demigod's arm. "You're scaring the children."

"Those aren't children," Castor spat. "They are the three women who set the fates of all beings—man, demigod, and god alike. They determine the lengths of our lives and the dates of our deaths. They are responsible for every shortened life, every person we loved who died early, every unjust death."

All three girls gasped, and Rowan, standing closer,

wrapped her arms around them. If glares could kill, there'd be a fried demigod on Greyson's wood floors right now. In a show of solidarity, Nefertiti suddenly appeared from wherever she'd been hiding and also placed herself in front of the girls, tail straight as a board, hissing a warning at the demigod.

"What is he talking about, Daddy?" The waver in Atleigh's voice broke his heart.

Leia tugged on Castor's arm. "They obviously don't know what you're talking about. Stop scaring them."

"There has to be some mistake." Marrok stepped forward now.

"Stay out of it, old friend," Castor snapped, not removing his eyes from the girls.

Greyson raised his hands, ready for whatever came his way. "Marrok's right. You've made a mistake."

"Do they join together in a trace?"

Holy hell. The blood shot to his feet, draining from everywhere else, leaving him lightheaded. *Could my daughters be fates?* Only, the things they talked about in that trance, more like they were talking *to* someone, not *about* them. It didn't fit.

But he couldn't focus on that now. Not with an enraged demigod standing before him.

Castor zeroed his gaze in on Greyson. "I know these women well. They killed my first wife. They've killed everyone I've ever lost."

By now the girls had started sobbing behind him. Greyson gathered what tiny amount of strength he had inside him, preparing to fight.

"Calm!" At Rowan's single word, a sense of serenity poured through Greyson, starting in his chest and moving out to his extremities like a river of peace and tranquility. He didn't lose sight of the danger, but the anxiety and adrenaline pumping through him moments before dissipated in the wake of the magic swirling through the room.

Castor, too, relaxed his stance, releasing his hands, which had been fisted. Even his blue eyes dimmed slightly. Behind him, the girls quieted.

"Whoa," Tala muttered. "That would be a handy trick with wolf shifter pups. Any time you want a job, you have a place with us."

Slowly Greyson turned to face his nanny, whose pink-tinted skin had gone sickly gray. Her hands, which she still held up, shook horribly. Rowan tossed Tala a wan smile. "No, thanks. Takes too much energy."

Still holding her spell, she leaned against the wall. "Now. We are going to discuss this calmly and rationally. Got it?"

She glared at Castor. "These girls were born almost thirteen years ago. Whatever argument you had with the fates, Chloe, Lachlyn, and Atleigh are *not* them. We don't know what their power entails yet, but you don't get to blame them for some kind of past life. Do you understand?"

How she managed those words with such force, given her visible exhaustion, Greyson had no idea.

She'd never looked more beautiful, putting her own health at risk to protect his children as though they were her own. But he couldn't help her—not until he knew his daughters were no longer in danger. He turned back to Castor. "They are my natural-born children. I was there to witness their first breaths." Even as he'd witnessed his wife's last. "You will *not* harm them."

Contrition and confusion warred in Castor's eyes for a long moment as he stared at Greyson's daughters, lips compressed, jaw working. "I apologize," the demigod finally said. Any remaining aggression visibly leaked out of him as his shoulders dropped. He addressed the girls directly. "Forgive me. You just...look exactly the same."

Leia snuck her hand into her husband's.

"Everyone okay, then?" Greyson spun at the sound of Rowan's hoarse whisper. "Good," she slurred. Then she dropped to the floor in an unconscious heap.

Thankfully, Castor moved with the speed his father, Zeus, had gifted him, catching her before her head hit the ground.

"Is she okay?" Tala asked from across the room.

Greyson knelt beside her, running a hand over her clammy skin. Thankfully, her breathing was steady and even. "She'll be fine after a few days of rest. Magic uses energy. She just used more than her abilities support."

"Daddy?" With Rowan's spell dissipating from the room, his daughters' temporary calm was evaporating in the face of confusion and terror. He rose and gathered them close, heart breaking again at the trembling he could now feel in each of their slight bodies.

Greyson looked to Marrok. "Can you take Rowan downstairs to her bed?"

He hated not being able to do it himself, the need to protect this woman all but screaming at him, but he had no choice.

"I'll take her," Castor offered.

Greyson shook his head. "No. We need more information, and, frankly, I don't trust you with her."

"Marrok and I will take care of Rowan," Tala said.

Castor grimaced but handed Rowan's limp form over to the alpha wolves without quibble.

"Why don't we all sit down?" Leia suggested.

"Good idea," Greyson said. "We need to know everything."

• • •

The magical alarm Grey had put on the girls at night and

grudgingly extended to include her woke Rowan from a deep sleep and a lovely dream where she and Grey had danced under the light of a full moon. Her body still ached from the burn of desire reflected in his eyes.

With a reluctant groan, she dragged herself out of the dream, only to gasp as memory returned in a rush of images.

The girls.

Grey.

The magic she'd used way too soon after her whole ghostly thing.

Oh my gods. How long have I been out?

But she couldn't think about that now. She needed to follow the girls. At least they were still breathing; that much was obvious if they were doing their sleepwalking bit. Limbs heavy and sluggish, Rowan managed to toss off her blankets and get out of her bed, stuck her feet into fuzzy slippers and pulled a ratty old sweatshirt on over her head. Cautiously, she made her way upstairs to find Grey waiting on the screened-in back porch with two steaming cups of coffee.

"No tea?" she asked.

"I didn't know if you'd wake up or not," he whispered through a smile. As he spoke, he trailed his gaze over her face. He held out a cup for her. The tender light in those dark eyes had to be a trick of the moonlight.

"How long have I been out?" she asked in sleep-hushed tones as she accepted her cup, curling her fingers around the warmth and inhaling.

His lips flattened. "Two days."

Well, damn.

Nothing could be done about it now. "Same place?" She waved toward the woods where the girls had gone last time.

Despite her warm sleepwear and thick sweatshirt, she shivered as his gaze licked over her. She wore layers of clothes, and suddenly she felt naked before him. Laid bare.

"Yes," Grey finally whispered. He held out his hand. "Ready?"

Rowan hesitated only a millisecond before she placed her hand in his. Immediately, the lines on her wrist heated up at his touch, though not in an uncomfortable way, more like an electric blanket plugged in and turned to high. With a tug Grey led her down the stairs to the frost-covered grass, then into the woods and up the incline of the mountain.

Rowan tried not to soak in how right her hand felt in his, how that small contact engendered a sense of safety and protection. Grey would take care of her.

What am I thinking? Grey was the hound the Syndicate had set on her trail.

Before she knew it, they arrived at the edge of the clearing where the girls had already gathered. Just like last time, the three stood in a circle, bathed in the pure light of the moon. They'd already started their swaying. The glow wasn't as much of a shock this time, as Rowan knew to expect it. However, their light still blinded her, painfully bright, even as silence descended.

Lachlyn's voice sounded this time, instead of Chloe's. "Rowan would never hurt us. She loves us."

Rowan jolted at the impact of those words. Fear spiking through her, she jerked away from Grey, snatching her hand out of his. At the same time, the lines on her wrist flared to horrible, burning life. She dropped to her knees, cradling her arm—which she sort of expected to be wreathed in flames, but wasn't—against her. Swallowing around the pain, which, once again, oozed out of her almost as quickly as it had come, she breathed through it. Finally, she glanced up at Grey who had dropped to crouch beside her, though he hadn't touched her. Scowling, jaw like stone, and a hard light in his dark eyes.

"You're going to kill me," she whispered.

A cry rose up inside her that she swallowed down even as

her heart shattered.

How could she have been such a fool? She'd let herself be lulled into a false sense of relationship with Greyson Masters and his daughters. But he didn't know the truth about her. When he did...

Grey reached out as if to draw her back. "Why would you say that? I could never kill you."

Rowan shook her head, her curls flying around her face. Randomly, she wondered when her appearance had been returned to normal. And by whom? Grey probably.

Focus! "They are the fates who predict death."

Still cradling her arm against her, she struggled to her feet, only to have Grey grab her arm. He pulled her deeper into the woods just as the girls drifted by. Their lovely faces still reflected the trance they entered to make their predictions.

She tried to tug out of his hold, but Grey wrapped his fingers around both arms now. "Look at me." He gave her a tiny shake.

Rowan glared up at him. "There's nothing you can say."

"They don't predict death. They aren't the fates."

She stopped herself mid-argument, mouth wide open. Wait. What? She narrowed her eyes, suspicion warring with ridiculous hope inside her. "What *do* they predict?"

He shrugged broad shoulders, almost a twitch. "Nothing. While you were out, we had Delilah's people examine them. They aren't fates."

"Then what are they?"

Now he hesitated.

"Spit it out, Grey." Please, nothing bad. For the girls' sake. For his.

He quirked his lips. "Did you know you're the only woman who talks to me like that? Most fall all over themselves to agree with me."

Rowan sniffed. "Your point?"

He grinned. "You're not very good for my ego."

"Maybe your ego needs taking down a peg."

Instead of answering, he shocked her by reaching for her wrist, which had at least dropped in pain levels, tingling now more than burning. "What happened to your arm?"

"Nothing." She tried to yank out of his grasp, but he held on. She knew the second he saw the lines—which were even more visible now, though they didn't make up an identifiable pattern—because he sucked in a sharp breath.

"Did you do this?"

She gritted her teeth against the accusation in his voice, in his shadowed eyes. "No."

"What happened, Rowan?" Something in his voice compelled her to answer.

"Some kind of magic gone horribly wrong." That, at least, wasn't a lie. She just didn't know what magic.

"Is it a burn?"

She tossed her hair back. Why not be honest. "That's what it feels like. The marks showed up when I arrived here."

There. You figure it out.

Grey's eyes widened. "Does it hurt now?"

Rowan shifted on her feet. Hurt? No. But with his continued touch, the tingling was gathering, fizzing through her blood and collecting heat at the juncture of her thighs. If he held on much longer, she might throw herself at him or orgasm on the spot. She wasn't about to share that tidbit of info. "Only when the lines brighten. They started out much fainter."

She gently tugged out of his grasp, sucking in a silent gulp of air as he allowed her to step back, and the sensations buffeting her body dissipated. "You still haven't answered my question. What are the girls, Grey?"

He stared at her for a long moment, gaze strangely intent. "We don't know yet."

That didn't make her feel any better. Especially given what they'd just been saying. She took a deep breath and looked him dead in the eyes. "I would never hurt them. *Ever.*"

"I know." Not even a smidge of hesitation. Grey tugged her in the direction of the house. "Come on."

Inside the house, he left her in the kitchen with a "don't leave" as he ran upstairs to check the girls. She stood, arms dangling at her sides, gaze focused on nothing in particular as thoughts chased themselves through her mind like hounds after a fox.

"They're fine," he said as he reentered the kitchen. The soft whisper still made her jump.

He sent her a smile she supposed was meant to soothe, but after tonight, and the warnings, and the way her heart was reaching for Grey and his family, it didn't help. If anything, the way he was trying to help only made this worse.

"Tea?" he asked, reaching for the cups in the cupboard.

I can't do this.

"Um…" She backed toward the door leading to her room. "Actually, I'm pretty tired. I think I'll just go to bed."

She tried not to see the surprise or acknowledge the disappointment that shadowed his face as she jerked the door open.

"Okay—"

Whatever else he was going to say was cut off by the sound of the door closing behind her.

Chapter Seventeen

He's going to figure it out.

She'd given too much away in those moments of both terror and heartbreak, thinking that he could kill her.

He had yet to question her, but he was too sharp not to figure out eventually that her level of fear made no sense unless she was harboring a secret that might put him in a position to have to punish her. Not to mention the girls' words.

Meanwhile the girls were stuck figuring out what their powers involved. The three discussed it endlessly.

"What if we're predicting people who meet each other?" Lachlyn wondered now.

Rowan glanced up from the green peppers she was stuffing for dinner. All three girls sat around the heavy wood kitchen table, halfheartedly practicing their magic.

"That would be dumb." Atleigh rolled her eyes. "And Delilah said we're not fates, so we're not predicting anything."

"We could be Seers," Lachlyn insisted.

"Yeah?" Chloe scoffed. "Predicting how a woman sets up a business she already has? Dad said she formed the business before we predicted anything."

Rowan silently agreed. That would be a waste of a Seer.

"Girls." As soon as she had their attention, Rowan pointed at their plants.

"This is so boring," Atleigh whined.

Persephone, displeased with their progress, had assigned them extra homework on top of what they had for school. More plant growing. Today the girls were making philodendrons sprout vines. Their aunt had assigned a specific length as a goal.

"This is going to take forever," Chloe grumbled.

No argument there. Why their aunt insisted on training them like witches half their ages, she had no idea. Rowan cocked her head, eyeing the plants. Maybe she could spice things up without going against the rules. "Give me a second to finish these. Then I'll show you a game."

"We can't play a game." Atleigh waved at her project. "We have to grow stuff."

Rowan allowed herself a delicate snort. "I'm well aware you can all grow those plants without a second thought."

The three froze and exchanged a glance. Rowan hid her small smile as she continued to prepare dinner.

"Aunt Persephone says we're not ready."

And who was Rowan, a lowly magic-lacking nanny, to say otherwise? "Have you told her you can do more? Or tried to show her?" She still hadn't figured out why the girls held back during lessons.

"Yes." Chloe scowled. "We got in trouble for trying to do *too much, too soon,* and *not following her instructions*."

Not for the first time, Rowan wondered what the other woman's play was. No way could she be a licensed instructor and have missed the girls' natural talents. Best guess, Persephone was slowing them down in order to ensure extra time with Grey, which would explain the vague stare of suspicion aimed Rowan's way every time she met the woman.

"What about your dad? Have you told him you can handle more?"

Again, exchanged glances told her they hadn't shared this with Greyson.

"He'll listen to Aunt Persephone. Not us," Atleigh said. Yup. Remembering this age, she probably wouldn't have told her dad, either. Or Tanya, as the case might be. Grey's job also kept him away. Not that he'd been away much since she'd arrived, but the girls alluded to it enough. Maybe a deeper level of trust needed to be established?

"I think you'd be surprised." Rowan chewed at her lower lip. How could she help them with that?

At their skeptical looks, she shrugged. "It's up to you, but you won't know for sure unless you try." She turned back to her dinner preparations and let them stew on that a moment. "Back to the plants. Since you're required to practice, maybe we can make it fun."

She topped the peppers off with fresh grated cheese, popped them in the oven, and set the timer before turning to face the girls. "Are you interested?"

"I guess," Lachlyn muttered, flicking the leaf of her plant with a finger.

"Right. Outside then. Bring your plants."

They followed her to the flat space of land behind the house before the tree line where the mountain inclined. Rowan inhaled appreciatively. Having grown up most of her life on the coast of Scotland, she was used to the bracing scent of sea air. Here the air was fresher in an odd way, with the zesty scent of pine subtly wafting on the breeze. The weather was also warmer here for this time of year, as Scotland sat farther north on the globe.

"Now, put your plants down in a line here." She drew a line in a patch of dirt with her foot.

Another round of pouting glances, but they did as she asked. Then, making a big thing of the act, Rowan paced from the line to a point farther away and drew another line with her foot.

"When I say go, shoot your growing vines this way. The first to the finish line wins a skip day."

The girls perked up, eyes brighter, backs straighter. "What's a skip day?" Chloe asked.

"A day when you don't have to go to magic practice after school. It'll have to be a day your dad can stay with you, or he can take the losers to practice and I stay with you."

Lachlyn slumped, arms crossed. "Dad will never allow it."

"Let me deal with your dad. I'm sure I can fix it." She wasn't all that sure, but she'd address the issue later.

Chloe suddenly grinned and rubbed her hands together and shot a very un-Chloe-like stare at her sisters. "You are going down."

"Don't you bet on it." Lachlyn switched from scowling to determined so quickly Rowan had to hold in a grin. "I'm going to win," the almost teenager declared.

"No way," Atleigh added, stepping up to her own plant, chin set in determination.

Rowan laughed, pleased to see them lose those morose expressions. "On three... One. Two. Three!"

With amazing speed, the vines for all three plants leaped forward. She'd known they could. Amazing what a little competition could do.

Rowan squealed with as much delight as the girls as their vines crept along the ground.

"Oh, no," Chloe wailed. "Mine's stuck on a weed and now it's growing up instead of out."

"Turn it around," Rowan yelled.

Meanwhile Atleigh and Lachlyn were neck and neck.

Lachlyn's glower of concentration was fierce as she scolded her plant, while Atleigh's approach was more encouraging.

Slowly, Atleigh's pulled ahead, until, finally her vine crossed the finish line first.

"Yes!" Atleigh jumped up and down.

"Dang," Lachlyn groaned.

Chloe, however, ran over to give her sister a hug. Then she turned to Rowan and flung her arms around her middle, squeezing her with an exuberant embrace. "That was fun, Rowan. Can we do it again?"

Rowan laughed. "If we grow those plants any longer, your aunt will think you cheated."

"What is going on here?" Grey's laughing voice interrupted their fun. They all jerked their gazes to find him standing by the door, arms crossed and with a fierce glower ruined by twitching lips.

A different man from the one she'd met the first day. That man would've been serious in his glowering. This one almost looked as though he wanted to join the fun.

"Rowan was helping us practice our magic by making it a race."

"I won, Dad!" Atleigh bounced over to him, tugging on his hand to pull him over to see.

After inspecting the results, Grey hugged Atleigh. "Good work. To all of you! Persephone will be pleased, I'm sure."

Gathering their plants, looping the tendrils of green-leafed vines over their arms, the girls giggled and chatted all the way back into the house.

"What did she win?" Grey asked.

Rowan pasted on her most innocent expression. She hoped it came across innocently, at least. "A skip day from magic practice."

He snorted a laugh. "I see."

She peeped at him from behind a fall of her hair. "You'll

allow it?"

"I shouldn't, but I haven't seen them that excited about magic in ages. Yes. I'll allow it."

That was easier than she'd expected. Rowan blew out a relieved breath and moved to follow the girls into the house, but Grey surprised her by stepping into her path, closing the door and leaning against it. "Did you stop to consider what might happen if their magic got out of hand? Heightened levels of emotion—including excitement—can trigger a spell to go horribly wrong."

Damn. She hadn't, because any magic gone wild she could handle. But that was the true Rowan, not weak-magic-user nanny Rowan. The question had been put gently, so she checked his expression, which gave her no clue as to his thoughts.

"Of course I considered that." *Think fast.*

His brows drew lower, while his gaze remained so intently on hers, it suddenly got more difficult to breathe. "Really? Because last time you used magic you turned pink."

If she hadn't known he was angry, the way he was looking at her might be interpreted as...

She cleared her throat, cutting that thought off. "I figured at worst you might have to dig your house out from under a mountain of philodendron vines. Worth the trouble if it got them more motivated. Don't you think?"

Did his lips twitch? "It's...nice...to hear them laughing so much again. Thank you for that."

Warmth slipped through her defenses and into her heart. She bit back an answering smile. At the end of the day, she shouldn't be getting so attached.

He studied her for a long moment, and Rowan resisted the urge to shuffle her feet, holding his gaze. He'd been doing that more since Lachlyn's words in the woods. Watching her.

"Your day off is tomorrow."

The comment came so far out of left field, it took her a moment to catch up. "Err... Yes."

"Do you have any plans?"

Where was he going with this? "I—"

"As it happens, work is a tad slow for me. With the girls at my parents', that leaves me free as well. Would you like to join forces?"

He wanted to spend the day with her? The part of her that quickened every time he entered the room, like the world had been dull and gray without him directly in view, the same part that right now reveled in the spicy scent of his aftershave and the woodsy scent she associated with his magic, screamed *Yes!* The cautious side, however, the side that worried over the fact that she had the strangest urge to confess all and put herself in Grey's capable hands, had her holding back.

Bad idea. Horrible. Delilah would kill her if the Syndicate didn't.

"Um. Thanks for the offer, but I already have plans." Damn. Did that sound as lame to him as it did to her?

"I see." His smile faded, and suddenly before her stood the intimidating warlock she'd first met when she'd arrived to be the girls' nanny.

"Maybe next weekend?" she tried.

But he didn't unbend. "It'll depend on my schedule."

Right. Had she hurt Grey with her casual rejection? The problem was, she couldn't put off her very real plans—not any longer—and she couldn't invite him along.

"I'll take the girls over to my parents' around eight. What time do you plan to leave?"

"About the same time." She pointed her feet toward the house, taking one reluctant step after another. "I'd better get inside now. Dinner's probably done baking."

"No more burned dinner fiascos?"

She glanced over her shoulder, surprised at the laughter

lurking in his voice, given his stoic reaction to her rejection moments ago. "It's easy when no one is messing with you."

He laughed outright, a deep, rich sound that shot straight to her heart. "I guess that does make things go smoother."

"You should do that more." The words escaped her guarded lips.

He cocked his head. "Do what?"

"Laugh."

His expression stilled, turning more serious, though warmth lingered in his dark eyes. "I have been…lately."

Lately as in since she'd arrived?

Stop wishing for things you can't have.

With a creak, Grey opened the screen door and held it for her.

"Thank you—"

As she glanced at him in passing, Rowan caught a glimpse of movement in the trees behind his right shoulder. Rather than draw Grey's attention, she turned and kept going, but she knew exactly what she'd seen. A large male elk, the rack on his head massive, stared at her from the shadows. Above him, perched on the branches of the tall pine tree, had to be at least twenty chipmunks, squirrels, marmosets, and birds of varying types, also staring her way.

Rowan's heart shriveled like a raisin in the sun.

Danger.

How could she have dismissed the hummingbird's warning so easily, distracted by Grey and the girls? But the question was, what danger? The Syndicate closing in? Something else?

It was never a good sign when animals started to gather around her in large numbers. The first time it happened, her parents were killed in a car crash she mysteriously survived. Tanya had speculated that was no accident but a Syndicate-sanctioned execution. Not that they'd ever found proof. The most recent time had been right before Kaios had showed up, killed Tanya—no mean feat—and kidnapped Rowan, using her, getting her into this mess in the first damned place.

The danger they'd been warning her of must be getting closer.

How long before Grey, or the girls, noticed the unusual behavior of the animals in their woods? And was Rowan the only one in danger? Or was something coming that could put this family—who'd already been through so much, and who'd managed to creep into her heart and take up permanent residence—in peril?

She'd find out tomorrow.

Chapter Eighteen

"Dad?"

Chloe's tentative question pulled Greyson's thoughts away from the red-haired, bewitching nanny who'd driven away in her beat-up Chevy that morning, earlier than she'd originally indicated. Rowan hadn't even paused to eat breakfast with them, though he'd made plenty. And despite the fact that the girls—whom he could tell had become quite attached to their nanny—begged her to. She hadn't said where she was going, or with whom, and he hadn't asked.

He should've. He'd damn well wanted to. That nagging sense something else was going on with her hadn't gone away. If anything, the girls' words that night had warning bells jangling inside his head. How the hell could she think he'd kill her? No mistaking the terror in her eyes. What had he done to warrant that kind of fear? His job, maybe, but that wasn't enough.

Her behavior since, had raised his concerns even more. She'd been…reserved. Not in a way he could put his finger on, no action to point to. Just a gut knowledge.

"Yes, Chloe?" he answered, slightly distracted.

"Do you think you could work with us on magic in the afternoons? Instead of Aunt Persephone?"

Greyson's attention moved fully to his daughters now. "My job doesn't give me consistent time at home. I know I've been around a lot lately, but things won't stay that way."

At their slumped shoulders, he put down his fork. "Why? Don't you like Persephone?"

"Oh, we love her," Lachlyn spoke up. "Just not her lessons."

Amusement tugged at his lips. "Why not?"

"She treats us like we're babies, Dad." Atleigh's put-upon sigh said more than the words.

"I'm sure she knows what she's doing. After all, Persephone teaches many of the children in the area."

Three eager expressions shut down and closed off, as they flopped back against their seats at the breakfast table.

"I told you Rowan was wrong," Lachlyn hissed at her sisters.

Greyson, about to resume his breakfast, paused, fork halfway to his mouth. "What does Rowan have to do with this?"

Chloe wrinkled her nose. "She told us to talk to you about our lessons with Aunt Persephone."

She did that? Why?

"Were you complaining to her about your aunt?"

"No!" Atleigh sent him an offended glower. "Rowan noticed how bored we were with our lessons and said to talk to you."

Slowly, Greyson leaned back in his chair. Had he missed something directly under his nose? Were the girls bored, and could they handle more? He'd assumed Persephone had things well in hand and honestly hadn't paid much attention. Too many other issues overwhelmed him when it came to raising his daughters alone, and he'd been happy to pass that part off to someone else.

Meanwhile, a warmth he didn't want to examine too

closely bloomed in the region of his heart. Rowan had enough faith in him to send the girls his way with this issue.

Of course she did, you dumb ass. She can't handle it on her own.

However, rather than address it with him, she had encouraged the girls to do so, helping build their trust in him. He'd have to thank her later, after he found out why she thought, even for a second, that he could kill her. Kiss her, yes. Step way over the line she'd drawn and do a hell of a lot more than that, yes. But harm her?

Gods, she must be a demon sent to torment him.

"I'll watch more closely tomorrow. Okay? And if she needs to increase the level, then I'll talk to her."

At least the girls perked up, resuming shoveling forkfuls of eggs into their mouths almost as fast as they could swallow.

"Oh, hey, Dad?" Lachlyn asked around a bite.

Again, he put his now cold bite of eggs down. "Yes?"

"I think Rowan likes you."

He was thankful he hadn't taken that bite, or he would've choked. He couldn't deny the burst of interest those words provoked. Now he was acting like a boy half his age with a first crush. But if she…

"I like her, too," he said casually.

And earned an eye roll from Atleigh for his trouble. "No, Dad. *Like*-likes you."

He shook his head. Dealing with his own thoughts in regard to his nanny was one thing. Encouraging the girls was another. "Rowan's just nice to everyone."

"She doesn't look at you like she's just being nice."

He paused with the fork raised yet again as something like hope—only it couldn't be that, could it?—surged through him. Now he was tempted to ask his juvenile daughters for more. This really had to stop.

"I doubt that—"

"Only when you're not looking," Chloe said.

"Don't tell her that," he said with a stern look. "She'd be horribly embarrassed. True or not."

Only, a growing part of him wanted it to be true. Wanted her to look at him the way a woman looked at a man she wanted. But more than that, a man she trusted.

And, after that night, he knew they weren't there yet.

· · ·

Rowan gazed over the vista laid out before her like a perfect painting. She'd pulled off at one of the many scenic overlooks along Trail Ridge Road, which traversed the Continental Divide. Technically, the road wasn't open to drivers yet—closed for the season—but as a witch who could teleport, Rowan wasn't too concerned.

Now, standing above the tree line, the windswept alpine tundra almost rolled away from her, though she knew full well that a bit farther on a life-ending drop awaited. Above her the slopes spiked away again to jagged peaks. She gazed to the west, to the heart of the Rockies, the crags and peaks rising across the horizon in an unending display of how puny humans were against such natural grandeur.

The animals she'd stopped and talked to along the way had directed her here. She shivered now, as the high winds penetrated her thin jacket. She'd been waiting here for forty minutes without a single animal appearing. Still, creatures worked on a different timetable than humans. So she continued to wait. She needed to know...

A falcon's cry pierced the air. However, a quick search of the sky revealed no bird near her. Again, the screech rent the morning silence, carried to her on the currents of the wind. Then, in a rush, the bird soared up from below, over the edge of the mountain and straight toward her. A whispered spell protected her delicate skin from her sharp talons, and Rowan held out her arm for the gyrfalcon to perch upon.

Wings flared wide to slow her approach, she gave several sharp flaps as she landed, then folded them neatly back. Beautiful with her white speckled belly and darker speckled wings, she cocked her head and regarded her with piercing yellow eyes.

"Rowan McAuliffe."

Her voice punched through Rowan's mind, surprisingly smooth.

"Yes. Can you tell me what danger follows me?" *Please don't let it be Grey. Please. Please. Please.*

The Syndicate wouldn't be much better.

The falcon bowed her head. *"Wolf shifters."*

Relief hit her first, like her lungs could suddenly expand. Not Grey. The danger wasn't him or the Syndicate. Half a beat later, the falcon's words sunk in, and dread burst inside her chest before sinking to the pit of her stomach.

She'd expected to hear the Covens had discovered her location under their very noses and were coming for her. But wolf shifters could mean only one thing. Kaios's helpers hadn't *all* been killed, and now they were coming for her.

"Who?"

"Kaios's lover."

Kaios had a lover? Hexes, hells, and parsnip. That woman. The one who'd taken pleasure in taunting her when Kaios hadn't been around.

That made a few things clearer, especially how he'd gathered a following of shifters. His lover must be one.

A she-wolf now bent on vengeance hunted her? Fan-freakin-tastic.

"How long before she finds me?"

"A few days. Maybe three at most. She hasn't caught your

scent yet. But she's close."

"Is she alone?"

"No."

"How many?"

"Unclear. Around ten."

Boiling cauldrons and pickled pig's feet. Too many to handle alone.

"Is there anything else I should know?"

"Call upon those you need when the time is right." With a leap that barely moved her arm, so light was the bird of prey, the gyrfalcon took to the skies, diving back over the cliff from which she'd come.

Now what did she mean by that last comment?

Long after the bird departed, she stared, unseeing, after it. What should she do?

Her first instinct screamed run. With wolf shifters on the warpath, her presence put Grey and the girls in danger. Given the power even a shifter could wield over her, the wolves could force her to hurt them.

She shouldn't stay. However, stay or not, her scent led the wolves directly to Grey's house, which meant they remained in peril even if she escaped.

Leaving them, leaving Grey—her heart ached at the prospect, like a thousand pinpricks all at once, leaving her bleeding inside. How had he become important to her in such a short time? No sense lay in the emotions with which she associated him.

She'd call Delilah, call upon the protection the woman, whatever she was, could provide Grey and the girls, not to mention she could bring in Tala and Marrok and their newly combined clan.

Her little family needed protection now.

After that, before the wolf shifters could pounce, Rowan would disappear.

Chapter Nineteen

At a tentative knock, Grey glanced up from his email to find Rowan standing in the doorway.

"I wanted to let you know I was home."

He leaned back in his chair, taking a moment to absorb how nice the word "home" sounded on her lips, taking in her appearance. She'd already kicked off her shoes. The woman seemed to have something against them. Her adorable toes scrunched into the thin carpet covering the hardwood of his office, like they protested his glance.

He lifted his gaze, trying not to also stare at that stubborn chin, or freckles, or lips that he wanted pressed against his. "Did you enjoy your day?"

"Yes." Her expression gave away little, but the slight tightening to her lips told him she'd rather not talk about it.

Curious, he let it go, nonetheless. "Good. Have you had dinner?"

Only a slight hesitation. "No."

"I make a mean spaghetti. Would you like to join me?"

A longer hesitation this time. What was with her all of a

sudden? Had dealing with Castor, and the physical toll that took, scared her, made her rethink working for him? His job did have the potential to bring danger, but he'd warded the house against outside threats. The thought of her leaving was as sharply unpleasant as a punch in the nose, making it hard to see straight through the sting.

The same sting her fear of him in the woods had brought. Only that had been worse. The fear in her eyes, the certainty that he'd cause her any harm. But how could he harm someone who'd become as important to him as she had? The girls trusted her, had come to rely on her. So had he. He couldn't do this without her. What's more, he didn't want to. When had that happened?

"That would be nice. Thank you."

Still recovering from his over-the-top reaction, Greyson glanced at his watch, more as a stalling tactic to gather his wits. He knew the time, as the day had moved in frustrating slowness. This had nothing to do with the witch before him, of course, just irritation with the lack of movement on his case and the strange quiet of an empty house. "Give me about an hour?"

"Do you need any help?"

He shook his head. "It's your day off."

A genuine smile lit her eyes. "So it is. I'll see you in an hour, then."

A few hours later, Grey poured the last of the wine into both their glasses and led Rowan to the couch in the family room. She walked through the corner of the room beside the fireplace and shivered.

"Cold?" he asked.

She smiled and lowered herself to the couch. "Something about that spot. It's always freezing."

"I know. It's been that way since…"

Why'd he pause? "Since?"

His lips tipped in a self-deprecating smile. "You'll think it's silly, but that spot showed up when my grandmother, Essie, died. I sometimes feel it around the cat, too."

"You're not the only one," Rowan murmured, glancing around surreptitiously. If Grandma Essie was a spirit, what did she think about all this?

And why didn't I see her that night I was in the spirit realm?

With a whispered spell from Grey, the fireplace blazed to life, casting a cheerful light over the night-darkened room.

All through dinner, Rowan had seemed hesitant with him—quieter than she normally tended to be, not looking him in the eye, a fact that bothered him more than he should let it. He'd spent most of dinner trying to convince himself that his feelings weren't as deep as they seemed and keeping the conversation impersonal and light, putting her at ease until she relaxed, but her tension had spilled over to him. He kept rolling his shoulders like that would help. It didn't.

Now, seated with one foot tucked up beneath her, she cast him a sideways glance, catching him watching the play of the firelight over her hair. He had to admit to a certain fascination at the way the dancing light burnished the tresses in alternating patterns of gold, dark red, and black.

He'd been doing that a lot lately. Watching her. He wanted to do even more. Only he was trapped between that need and who she was to his family. But he couldn't look away now. Idly he wondered if her hair would feel as silky against his fingers as he thought. The image of her tresses spread out over a pillow or across his chest had him sucking in a sharp breath.

He curled his fingers around the stem of his wineglass to keep from reaching out for her. "What did you end up doing today?"

Wrong thing to say. Rowan lowered her eyes, her

expression turning guarded. "I went hiking."

Greyson took a swallow of wine as he considered why hiking would be a wary subject for her. "Where?"

"Off Trail Ridge Road."

Ah, where he'd suggested taking her. Ignoring the bite of what that meant, Greyson tried to flash a teasing grin. "If you didn't want to spend the day with your boss, all you had to do was say so."

Her hands twisted in her lap. What was wrong with her? "It wasn't that—"

Enough.

Grey plonked his glass down, lucky he didn't break it with the force, and sat forward so he could reach across the space between them. He put a hand over hers, which twisted in her lap. "Do I make you nervous, Rowan?"

She whipped her head to stare at him, both wary and surprised. "No."

Liar. "So it's my position as your boss? Or maybe with the Syndicate?"

"Not your position exactly..." Now she was hedging. "More what you do. I imagine you must be a powerful warlock to be the lead hunter for the Syndicate."

"I would never use my power against you, Rowan. I hope you know that."

A flash of emotion, something he couldn't pin down, but which had his gut twisting like her hands had been, was there then gone. Replaced by what he was convinced was a deliberate cheeky grin, the same one that had stolen his breath the day she walked into the house unannounced, past all his wards, and spelled his daughters. "You couldn't risk losing another nanny."

Compelled by the teasing dancing in her eyes and the need to take and keep that smile for his own, Greyson scooted across the couch, closer to her, allowing her wildflower scent to wash over him. Rowan's eyes widened at his nearness, though he didn't touch her beyond his hand over hers. This close, even by the dim light of the fire, he could see flecks of blue in the gray irises. What would she do if he kissed every one of those freckles across the bridge of her nose? "I mean it. You will always be safe with me."

Instead of relief or trust, a deep sadness fell over her expression like a storm racing across the sky, blocking the glow of the sun. And fear. Just before she closed her eyes, shutting him out. On the heels of a sensation akin to a punch to the gut, a fierce, protective instinct surged through him with a strength that shocked the hell out of him. But before he could say more, she closed the distance between them. Surprise held him immobile as she pressed her lips sweetly to his.

A thank-you. That was all. He knew that, could feel it.

He wanted to sink into the kiss, plunder her mouth, and possess her body, while at the same time cherishing everything she was. But she pulled back before he could act, eyes still closed.

"You're a good man, Greyson Masters."

Why was she using his full name? She only ever called him Grey.

Rowan opened her eyes, wariness darkening the color to storm. "But you don't know me. I'm...trouble."

Sensing she wouldn't welcome the desire slamming through him, he held his emotions in check, even as questions swirled through his mind. Lifting a hand, he gently tucked a tendril of hair back from her face, noting its soft texture against his fingertips.

Silk. I knew it. "I could use more trouble in my life."

A laugh burst from her, warming his heart. He could use more of that, too. Laughter.

"Chasing down magic offenders and keeping track of

triplets who go into the woods in a trance isn't enough trouble for you?" she asked.

The question was teasing, but he didn't miss how she scooted away from him, putting distance between them.

He wanted to pull her back but made himself chuckle lightly instead. "I guess not."

"I hope I'm not interrupting anything?"

An ice-cold mountain spring had nothing on the sound of Persephone's voice intruding on the moment.

"Aw, hell and hexation." Though he doubted his sister-in-law did, he caught Rowan's whispered expletive as she stood, scooping up her wineglass. "Not at all. I was about to go to bed anyway."

His wife's sister regarded them with narrowed eyes. "Yes. It certainly looked like it."

"Persephone." He deliberately imbued the word with warning.

She blinked, and suddenly her expression shifted from poisonously suspicious to pleasant. He almost wondered if he'd been wrong about her attitude. Almost.

"I thought you might be lonely with the girls away and came over to keep you company." She glanced at Rowan's departing back as she scurried away to the kitchen. "I guess I should have come sooner."

He made a show of glancing at his watch. "It's a bit late. But we'll see you tomorrow when you come for the girls."

The soft *click* of a door in the kitchen told him Rowan had gone down to her rooms without saying good night. *Damn.*

Determination not to leave things where they were drove him off the couch. Only he had to get Persephone out of the house first.

And then what?

He had no idea. But he'd figure it out.

Chapter Twenty

With shaking hands, Rowan stripped off her clothes and dressed in her favorite tank top and flannel pajama pants. What on earth had she been thinking, kissing Grey like that? Spending the evening with him, fantasizing that she was exactly the person she pretended to be and the desire she couldn't miss in his gaze, in his touch, was something she was allowed to act upon.

The ache in her heart had turned into a torment. Each word, each moment shared felt like the tip of a knife slipping between her ribs and twisting, because she knew she had to go. Gods, she'd been tempted to take him up on the offer the heat in his eyes had been making.

Just one night together. Something to remember…

What would he say if she told him the truth?

Not who she was, but the fact that his mere nearness had her body humming with a strange electricity, a slow burn of desire that sizzled under the surface every time he appeared. Her body didn't do that with other men, even previous boyfriends.

She rubbed at the heat branding the inside of her wrist. The lines there had been on fire all night. She flipped her hand over and gasped. The faint white lines had solidified and come together, now appearing more like a tattoo, the design clear. A sigil, simple and flowing, the design was fascinating. If she guessed correctly, the sign was the sigil for the house of Masters.

"Magi by damned," she whispered in a broken voice.

The only sigil marks that showed up like a tattoo were those of a bonding—the mark a witch and warlock shared a sacred magically created connection. A vow.

Shifters tended to rely entirely on a fate bond for mating. But the occurrence among mages was possible through magic. Only many didn't take the option. Love and trust had to be unquestionable, because the act could change their magic.

Only wouldn't they have had to both agree to the spell?

Besides, Grey had said nothing. He had barely noticed shocking her when he'd touched her the day they met, and this mark had taken time to form. Therefore, this couldn't be a bonding. Could it?

She had three fucking days to clear out of here and draw the wolves hunting her away from Grey and the girls. What were the fates thinking? She'd ask the girls, but they still had no clue what they were predicting or why.

A bonding? Now?

This must be something else. It *had* to be.

But the only person she could ask would be Grey himself.

Rowan shook her head. No. She'd concentrate on her plan and deal with the wolf shifters. Then she'd confess everything to Grey and put herself in his hands. And…after all that…if this mark remained and he hadn't killed her, she would ask him about it.

But not before.

She startled as Nefertiti wound around her ankles,

rubbing against her in a show of comfort. Absently, Rowan reached down to pet her soft fur. "What am I going to do, Nefti?"

Nefti turned up her little pink nose and began washing herself, and Rowan shook her head. Like most cats, Nefti didn't deign to talk to a human. Even one she liked.

That cold chill passed through her body, shaking a shiver down her spine, snapping her out of her thoughts.

Right now, she needed help. Rowan hopped off her bed and snatched her purse from where she'd dropped it on the floor when she'd come home earlier. She fished out her cell phone and called Delilah.

"Rowan?"

"I'm in trouble, and I need your help."

"Is it Greyson?"

"Not the way you think." Quickly, Rowan explained the falcon's warning.

"We need to get you out of there. Now."

Rowan's heart, already heavy, dropped into her stomach. She'd known that was the answer, but the thought of leaving Grey, leaving the girls... She closed her eyes and took a deep breath. There was no other way.

"What if that leaves Grey and the girls vulnerable? They don't know danger is coming. I should tell Grey—"

"No. Not yet."

Rowan frowned at her phone. "Why do you say that?"

"Let's just say I have a Seer on staff. If Greyson finds out who you are now, things won't work out."

Rowan swallowed, that knife twisting deeper into her heart. Did that mean she'd die? Could Grey really kill her?

I'm a damn fool for ever thinking love could've been at the end of this twisted yellow brick road.

She didn't ask for clarification. She didn't want to know. They had more immediate issues. "I need to make sure they're okay."

"I could call Tala and Marrok, have them surround the place."

As much as the idea of fighting fire with fire appealed, Rowan couldn't ask the wolf shifter couple to help her again. They'd already done too much for a witch who technically attacked them. Besides… "More wolves might attract Kaios's lover. She'll want retribution against them, too. Warn them, but don't send them. Can we lay a false track for me, like you did from that cabin in the woods? Draw the wolves away from Grey and the girls?"

"Yes. That's possible. I can't guarantee they'll go for it. It's not foolproof."

"Okay." Rowan thought hard. "I'll drive out of here and teleport back."

"That won't work. The shifters will still sense your presence if you return. And you risk them controlling you. If Kaios had a lover no one knew about, she must be powerful."

"They won't sense me if I'm a wraith."

She'd hide herself in the spirit realm, again, like she had when she'd kept Grey from seeing all those memories correctly. As long as she didn't use her magic while in that form, she should be okay for a few days at least. She could watch over Grey and the girls, at least for a short while, to assure herself of their safety. Despite the trepidation that shook her at the thought of returning to that numb place, she had to do this. She couldn't remain that way for longer than four days, just to be safe, as Tanya had said five, without risking becoming permanently spectral. No magic would discover her, and no wolves could control her from the nether world.

"Are you sure?" Delilah asked.

For Grey and the girls, the risk was worth taking. "Yes."

"Okay. While you're doing that, I'll do my own hunting."

Rowan assumed that meant going after the wolves themselves with whatever means were at Delilah's disposal. Hopefully, this issue could be handled.

"After this is over, I'm telling Grey everything." She'd turn herself in to Grey and the Covens Syndicate and pray they didn't kill her before they questioned her.

"Let's see how everything goes first. I'll...have a chat with my Seer."

"Fine." Regardless of the Seer, she'd tell him the truth. Love had to start with trust. After she told him the truth, that might never happen for him, but she had to try. "Thank you, Delilah."

"Good luck."

Rowan hung up and tossed her phone on the bed. She needed to pack and disappear. But first, she had to tell Grey she needed to leave.

She hurried up the stairs. The house lay peacefully quiet, and she didn't bother to turn on any lights as she moved on silent bare feet through the halls, moving quickly at a half run.

And slammed into a solid chest as he stepped out of his room—bare, warm, and muscled if her fingertips told the truth. "Grey," she gasped.

Time suspended as they locked gazes. As if the moments between when she'd had her mouth on his and now hadn't happened. Only he did nothing, though his fingers curled around her arms tightened with each passing tick of the grandfather clock. The need undeniable. And dammit, she didn't want to keep rejecting it. Rejecting him. Because...

"Kiss me, Grey. Please."

In answer he yanked her into his arms and crashed his mouth upon hers, taking her lips in a searing kiss. Her body flared to glorious life under his touch. With a bold tongue, he demanded, and she gave everything he asked, opening to him, matching him thrust for thrust, every thought of what she needed to do fleeing her mind as liquid heat rushed through her in a lava flow of need.

He pulled back with a sharply indrawn breath. "Thank the gods. I was coming down to you. You feel it, too, don't you? This thing between us."

Her chore pushed aside by blazing need, which demanded nothing less than surrender, she nodded. "Yes. But I thought…Persephone?"

He shook his head. "I never encouraged her."

Thank the gods. Rowan hated the idea of him with that stuck-up witch.

He brushed a strand of hair back from her face, then leaned in to nuzzle her neck. "Stay with me tonight?"

One night just for her, for them—that was all she could give.

Again, she nodded, even as she stood on tiptoe, seeking his lips with her own. "Yes," she whispered against his mouth, and he crushed her to him.

Backing her up, Grey pressed her against a wall, his body solid and warm, pinning her there while his mouth ravaged hers. With a surprisingly light touch that sent shivers cascading over her skin and down her spine, he traced down her arms with both hands, then in a sudden move, took her by the wrists and pinned her hands above her head.

Rowan cried out as the sigil on the inside of her wrist, already on fire, flared to excruciating life at his touch. Heat flooded her blood and through her body to the throbbing juncture at her thighs.

Sweet heaven above, he might make her come simply by touching that mark.

Holding her arms with one hand, he trailed his other hand down to cup the heavy weight of her breast. Rowan gasped as her nipples peaked eagerly, seeking his touch even through her T-shirt.

"So sensitive," he murmured against her lips, satisfaction tingeing the words.

In answer Rowan tugged at her wrists, asking him to release her, then snuck her hand between them to where his hard length pressed against the zipper of his jeans. She stroked down the ridge of his erection, eliciting a groan.

"Mmmmm. So sensitive," she echoed his words, right down to the tone of satisfaction. And then took it a step further. "I wonder if it would be just as sensitive if I licked?"

She caught the white flash of his grin in the moonlit hallway. "Witch."

Before she could respond, he claimed her lips again, branding them his as much as the mark on her wrist did. Could she deny now the sigil was a bonding mark? Did she want to?

"Grey," she whispered between kisses.

"Yeah?"

"Take me to your bedroom."

She didn't have to tell him twice. Rowan gasped as he scooped her into his arms. With a well-placed kick of his foot, he knocked the door to his room open and marched across the floor. But, instead of rushing through the next moments, he slowly lowered her to the bed, the look in his eyes—intense, needy, and demanding—stealing her breath. No one had ever looked at her with such…adoration. She swallowed against the swell of emotion his gaze pulled out of her.

"You're so damn beautiful," he murmured, his low voice humming through her.

Forgetting herself, unable to resist the urge…resist him… anymore, she whispered a quick set of words. In an instant, their clothes disappeared, leaving them naked, the cool air against her heated skin only adding to the sensuous pleasure that held her in its grip.

Grey laughed. "And so damn surprising."

He leaned in to her, the weight and warmth of his body against hers, skin against skin, hard against soft, rough against silky smooth, delicious. "I didn't see you coming, but I'm happy you are part of our lives."

A stab of guilt arrowed through her but dissipated as he took her lips once more. He explored her with agonizing slowness, each caress, each taste of her deliberate and savored, driving her need for him higher and higher.

At the same time, she explored every inch she could reach, reveling in the hard, hot body under her fingertips, under her mouth. Gods, he smelled amazing, all pine and musk and man.

He moved down her body and took one pink nipple between his teeth, tugging gently, shooting sparks to her core and her wrist.

Rowan moved against him restlessly. "Grey," she moaned. And hoped he got the message. She needed him. Now.

"I know," he murmured against her breast. "I feel it, too."

He moved between her legs, positioning himself at her entrance. A spell whispered between his lips, protecting them both without the need for a condom, a bonus of being a witch. Then he pushed inside her slick heat in one long, slow move.

Rowan gasped as he filled her, the pressure sending her to a space in her head that turned almost floaty.

"You okay?" he asked.

"Yes. Gods, yes," she moaned.

Grey flashed a grin, then took her hands and positioned her arms above her head. Gazing deeply into her eyes, he started to move, pumping into her, lighting already sensitive nerves on fire with each thrust.

Rowan lost herself in his dark gaze, in the sensations flowing through her. She couldn't hold back the small sounds of pleasure keening out of her. Grey's own groans mingled with hers as he started moving faster.

Her orgasm came up on her fast, tingling low and then exploding out from there. Lights flashed behind her eyes in a dance of color as pure ecstasy shot through every nerve in her body. At the same time, Grey threw back his head with a shout, his body jerking as he spilled into her. The mark on her wrist burst with a pleasure so intense it spiraled her body into a second orgasm that went on and on.

And every moment she drowned in the possessive need staring down at her from Grey's eyes.

Once her body stopped shuddering, Grey pulled out, another spell cleaning them both up, then pulled her into his arms, yanking the covers over their hips. He laid a soft kiss on her shoulder as she sighed into the fading bliss, her body languorous and replete.

The afterglow of making love with Grey had Rowan unwilling to move. His heart thudded steadily beneath her cheek, the sound strangely comforting, reassuring.

Unable to help herself—the compulsion to touch too strong to ignore—she traced a fingertip over the tattooed sigil of his family name over his heart—this one a normal tattoo in black ink. The design matched the white lines on the inside of her wrist, which showed with even more clarity. No way could she deny the mark on her arm was his family sigil now. But hopefully he hadn't seen the glow. She couldn't show him. Not when she was about to do a disappearing act, taking the threat of attack with her.

"You truly are a witch, Rowan McAuliffe."

She smiled at his words, even as she reveled in the shiver his deep voice caused to ripple over her nerves. "Oh?"

"I don't lose control like that. Ever."

Surprise at his admission had Rowan lifting her head. She caught a flash of shock in Grey's eyes and grinned, pure feminine triumph thrumming through her. "I guess you kind of like me."

He gave his head a shake, lips tugged down in rueful amusement. "I hope that's obvious." He indicated their naked forms with a wave, then cupped her jaw with his hand, ensuring she looked him in the eyes. "What's more...I trust you."

Forget a slow twisting knife. Guilt lanced through her on a spike of pain, impaling her and stealing her happiness. And the smile fell from her lips. "You shouldn't."

Taking the sheets with her, embarrassed about her exposed state now, she sat up. Grey's eyes darkened as he took in both her verbal and physical rejection. "Rowan?"

She grimaced and rushed through what she had to say. "I talked to Delilah tonight."

He scooted up in bed, and she had to clench her hands to keep from reaching out to touch the enticing ridges of his stomach. "Oh?"

She licked dry lips. Now that the time had come, she dreaded what she had to do. But she had to. However, the excuses she'd come up with earlier seemed trite now. After what they'd shared, Grey deserved the truth. But telling him at this moment would result in one of two unsavory results. Either he'd turn her over to the Syndicate, or he'd insist on protecting her himself.

No. She'd deal with Kaios's lover and her shifters, with Delilah's help, and then she'd admit all. Stick to the plan.

However, she couldn't tell him the plan naked, because she suspected a hasty exit would be in order. Scooting off the bed, sheet wrapped around her toga style, she gathered her clothes strewn about the room, thanks to her earlier spell, and set about getting dressed. Grey watched in silence, not moving from where he lay on the bed.

Finally, she turned to face him, chin jutted out. "Delilah is going to be sending you a new nanny." She gave a regretful smile. "A…better one."

Grey jerked upright, eyebrows drawn down in a scowl. "What are you talking about? You're perfect for the girls. For m— For our family."

Rowan shook her head hard, backing up, her hair flying wildly about her face, and she probably resembled a banshee. "Delilah has an urgent need for me with…another family. Something she insists only I can handle."

Grey moved. Unashamed of his undressed form, he jumped out of the bed and pulled his jeans on, leaving the top unbuttoned. Even now, she itched to shuck them back off his body and tumble them both back into bed.

He moved in front of her and gripped her arms. But he didn't face her with anger now, only concern. "What could be so urgent a witch with limited magic could fix it? Let me help. Leaving here is not the answer."

Hounds of hell, this was harder than she'd anticipated. "I gave her my word."

He gave her a little shake. "You gave *me* your word. The girls will be devastated."

Tears pressing against her eyes, Rowan held on to the knowledge that what she was doing was for the girls' protection. "I'm hoping it'll be for only a few weeks. Then… we'll see." He wouldn't want to keep her around then anyway.

Grey released her arms, his falling limply to his sides. "So…you're not leaving forever. Only for a few weeks to help out Delilah."

If he'd accept that story, then… "Yes."

He huffed out a laugh, running his hand through his hair. "Sorry about that. I thought you meant—"

She shook her head, hiding her misery. "My fault. I wasn't clear."

He bent and retrieved his shirt, pulling it over his head. "When do you leave?"

Rowan swallowed. "In the morning. Early, since I have to drive. My...er...backup should arrive in a few days."

Breath punching from him, he reached for her, tugging her into his arms to rest his chin on top of her head. Releasing her own pent-up breath, she relaxed into him, soaking in his solid presence, the mark on her arm warming in a comforting way, like a cozy cup of tea by the fire. Only it couldn't last. When he found out...

Grey's deep tones rumbled under her cheek. "I would suggest we spend the rest of the night making love, but if you're driving, you should sleep."

Disappointment wanted to drown out her common sense. That voice of reason growing more and more faint under the cacophony of her clamoring needs. "Yeah."

"Stay with me?"

She screwed up her face. "I don't think that's a good idea."

He held up a hand, oath style. "Just sleep. I swear."

No way was she denying herself that luxury or the precious memory of sleeping in his arms. "Okay."

Leaving their clothes on, they lay down, wrapped up in each other.

"Sleep," he murmured, pressing a soft kiss to her forehead.

To her utter surprise, she did, absorbing every moment she had in his arms and doing her best not to think about tomorrow.

Chapter Twenty-One

The horrid sensation of passing into the realm of the dead was worth it, even with the pit of dread in her stomach. Back in that muted world sooner than she would've liked—hell, she could never like coming here—Rowan set herself up on a constant patrol of the house and grounds. For three days and three nights, she'd prowled, waiting for any sign her efforts to divert the trouble headed this way had failed.

The good news about being a ghost was she needed no sleep. No food. Tanya had never quite explained what happened to her physical body while she went all haunted. She'd be exhausted when she came out of it again, that much was clear. With each passing day, her form on this plane got lighter, less attached to her physical body if she had to hazard a guess. She could wait only one more day before pulling out of this spell.

"You're here to help my grandson?"

The voice, barely above a harsh whisper in the silence that reigned in this place, still had Rowan spinning around in search of the source. Her movement too quick, it took her hovering, translucent form a moment to catch up, swirling through the air in the strangest of ways.

The pale version of an old woman stood in the corner of the family room, close to the fireplace.

"Who are you?"

"I'm Esther Masters, Greyson's grandmother on his father's side. You may call me Essie. You don't have to tell me who you are, Rowan McAuliffe. I know everything. The girls told me."

The girls?

Realization hit with the subtleness of a cleaver to the head. "They're talking to you when they go into that trance?"

Essie shrugged. "Me. Other spirits who come to settle some things."

Mediums? The girls spoke to spirits. Delilah's people had been right, they weren't fates.

Rowan blinked as Essie's words sank in. Wait. What exactly did *everything* cover?

"Do you stand there often?" Rowan asked, thinking back to those times a shiver had slipped over her skin in that spot. "Or with Nefti?"

Essie—dressed surprisingly casually in trousers and a pale blouse, her short gray hair fluffed out in a halo around her head—gave a gleeful smile. "I do like making my presence felt, and cats have always been able to speak to the dead. It's why she's still my cat."

Rowan snorted a chuckle. "I see."

"She likes you, though."

They shared a smile of mutual amusement.

Getting no negative vibe from Grey's grandma, she relaxed slightly. "To answer your question, yes. I'm here to… check on…Grey and the girls."

Essie stared at her for a long, disconcerting moment. "You mean you're here to protect them from the wolves."

If Rowan had been attached to her body, she would've stumbled back in shock. Even so, her form shuddered, reverberating in a manner that caused a lance of pain through her head. How was that possible? More importantly... "How did you know?"

Essie smirked. "The animals aren't the only ones who pass on gossip. Ghosts are worse than men in a locker room, given they've nothing better to do than sit around watching the living."

Rowan had no idea where to go first with her questions. "Why not pass on, then?"

Another eerie stare from once-blue eyes, now strangely pale in Essie's face, made Rowan want to shuffle her feet like a truant schoolgirl. "Something told me my family needed some looking after."

What reply could she give to that? "Fair enough."

Grey chose that moment to enter the room. With automatic actions, almost as though his mind was a thousand miles away, he set the kettle to boiling and got out the tea. Only, when he opened the tin, he looked closer, then cursed. She'd forgotten to fill it back up before she left.

Flipping the stove flame off, he yanked out his cell phone and dialed. Judging by his dark scowl, Grey was not happy. Because of tea?

"Where is she, Delilah?" he barked without saying hello first. "I want to speak to her."

Delilah's reply came across too softly to catch the words, but Grey's glower deepened. "That's not good enough."

He paused, listening. Then he ran a hand through his hair, spiking it up, and Rowan lifted a hand only to drop it back to her side as his shoulders drooped forward in defeat. "You don't understand. You *need* to get her back here."

He blew out a long breath as he rubbed at his chest, then turned and headed back to his office.

"Because I love her, dammit. That's why." The words floated back to Rowan down the hallway. "I need her more than anyone else could possibly…"

Even here where everything—sensation, emotion, life—felt far away, a pale reflection like her form, a multitude of emotions slammed through her, lighting her up and dragging her down at the same time.

Had he just—?

Did he really say—?

Rowan turned to Essie, who still hovered in the corner. "Did…did you hear that?"

The old woman rolled her eyes. "You're both hopeless. But that's not what you need to worry about right now."

Despite the numbness of the realm, a trace of that prickly sensation walked down the back of her neck. Only one other thing could be more important. "The wolves are still coming?"

"They're not coming."

Rowan practically floated to the roof with relief.

"They're here." Essie pointed out the window.

Light flared outside, illuminating the dark, an instant before a series of explosions from outside boomed, splitting the silence with a crash of sound. The windows shattered, glass flying everywhere. The reverberations slammed through Rowan like shockwaves, even in the ethereal realm. Immediately, heavy black smoke poured into the room.

Upstairs, one of the girls screamed.

• • •

Grey shook his head as his ears rang following the blast. His lungs screamed in protest at the heavy smoke, his eyes watering. His house was under attack.

The wards would hold off whatever was out there, but not

indefinitely.

I have to get the girls to the panic room.

He'd save his magic for when he absolutely needed it. Most likely multiple assailants were involved, and the possibility of them being magical was high. He needed to preserve his energy. Even small spells would reduce his ability to fight, weaken him, and leave him vulnerable.

He sprinted through the house and up the stairs, shouting as he ran. "Girls!"

Immediately, doors were thrown back, and he sucked in a big breath of relief as all three appeared.

"Dad! What's happening?" Atleigh cried.

"Get them out of here, Grey." Rowan's voice echoed in the hallway, bouncing off the walls and making the hairs on the back of his neck stand up, his heart shrinking in on itself.

"Rowan?" Lachlyn asked, glancing around.

So he wasn't the only one who'd heard her.

Suddenly, the ghostly image of the woman he loved materialized before his eyes. See-through in grays and whites, her long hair floated around her head almost as if she were underwater.

What. The. Hell? Panic stronger than anything he'd ever felt left him reeling. "Rowan?"

She grimaced. "There's no time to argue or explain. There's a group of wolf shifters attacking. They are after me, not you. Get the girls to safety. I'll do what I can to hold them off."

Before he could stop her, she disappeared.

"Daddy?" Chloe's trembling voice pulled him back to the most important task.

"Downstairs to the panic room. Move."

Another round of explosions rocked the house as they hurried. He had to grab Atleigh, as a violent shudder sent her tumbling down.

With more haste than calm, he ran them to the kitchen, down Rowan's stairs, to the door hidden on the wall opposite the windows. With a whispered word, the door appeared. He quickly punched in a series of numbers in a keypad, and, with a *thunk*, the bolt slid back, and the door swung open.

"Get inside and don't come out until I tell you to or someone you know comes for you."

"You're leaving us?" Lachlyn screeched, even as she followed her sisters inside.

The three most precious faces in the world peered out at him, fear dilating their pupils, their bodies visibly trembling.

"The wards will withstand only so much, but a magical alarm was automatically triggered. Help is coming." Fast, he hoped. The problem with teleporting was it could be intercepted by magical means. He had no idea if the werewolves had another mage helping them, but he couldn't risk teleporting out. And the witches and warlocks coming to help would have to teleport somewhere a decent distance away and cover the rest of the way on foot.

"I have to hold them off until then. And if Rowan is out there…"

"Go, Dad," Atleigh said. "Don't let them kill her."

A swell of pure love kicked him in the gut. With a muffled exclamation, he leaned in and gave each of his daughters a kiss. "Even if they get by me and into the house, they shouldn't be able to get into this room. Even then, your mother's kiss of protection will keep you safe."

Gods above and below, torn didn't begin to describe his emotions. But leaving his daughters safe in the magical room built into the solid granite of the mountain while he went to keep the attackers out was his only choice.

"I love you. Always."

With that, he whispered the words that shut and locked the door and hid it from sight.

• • •

Rowan's only thoughts involved keeping the wolves out. The problem was, she had to remain a ghost or risk the shifters controlling her and using her to get past Greyson's wards inside. With a thought, pure will creating action, she forced her spectral form to disappear and reappear outside.

Remaining unseen, she took stock of the situation. Three wolves—massive in their animal forms, one gray and two red—stood facing the back of the house. Catching glints here and there, she could tell more remained concealed by the trees beyond. Knowing how this attack was going from the inside, she'd guess more still surrounded the house from all four sides to ensure no one got out easily.

Okay. Time for distract and disturb. Rowan had no idea if what she was about to try would even work. But people saw ghosts all the time, right?

Thinking solid thoughts, she willed her ghostly form to materialize to the attackers. The act required a huge amount of concentration and the unpleasant sensation akin to being underwater after the air in her lungs ran out. Finally, she thought she'd achieved it, based on what she could see of her more solid-looking form.

"I'm here," she called. "I'm the one you want."

The three wolves closest to her turned with a snarl. *Guess it worked.*

One of the red wolves leaped at her, and she allowed her form to disappear. Not difficult. Holding herself as a visible entity had taken effort. Her body wanted to be invisible, to no longer exist.

The creature flew through the air and slammed into the pine tree behind where she'd appeared. The tree, on the skinnier side, cracked and split with the impact, and pine needles rained down like dry water as the upper half fell to the ground with a crash of limbs, pinning the wolf beneath it.

His companions didn't bother to check on him. Instead they let out twin howls, which Rowan, as an Aneval, easily translated into, *"She's here. Bring reinforcements."*

A midnight-black female wolf sprinted from around the side of the house, followed by three others. Those inside the tree line remained where they were as far as Rowan could tell. As the female neared, the big gray wolf suddenly shifted, his body shimmering like a mirage with the change as bone realigned and fur receded into skin, clothing appearing, until before her stood a man with gray at the temples and a nasty scar running down the side of his neck.

"She is here, mistress." He addressed the black female wolf, slightly smaller in form than most of the others.

Kaios's lover. Rowan had seen her only in human form before.

The red wolf with him—the one still standing, at least—growled, and Scar Neck grimaced.

"That is, there's a ghost that *looks* like the McAuliffe witch here."

The hackles raised on the black wolf's back, and she bared her teeth in a silent display of displeasure.

Before Rowan could hear more, the sensation of ice being wrapped around her neck invaded her form an instant before she was yanked back into the house.

Rowan took a second to shake off the splinters of cold remaining inside her, even as she wondered what the hell had just happened to her.

Essie, likely tired of waiting for her to reorient, shoved her face in front of Rowan's. "Grey is outside."

"What?" Rowan tried to whip her head around, though her floating form took a second to keep up. Still, he was nowhere in sight. "Where?"

"Out front. He's protecting the girls...and you."

Fear shot through Rowan like a bolt of electricity.

Before she could do more, another howl went up outside, followed by a low rumbling she took a second to identify as a growl. From all the wolves. If she'd been in her corporeal form, the hairs on her arms would've stood up at the terrifying sound.

A blinding flash of blue lightning split the night sky, preceding a slam of thunder so deafening it seemed to shake the entire mountainside.

Grey.

The cacophony of fighting reached her in an odd reverberation of sound, like hearing the noise through a tunnel.

"Follow me," Essie said.

Rowan floated after Grey's grandmother to the windows showing the back yard. "They're in the woods now. I can go no further. My spirit is tied to this house. You must help him. Protect him."

Already, Rowan's life force ebbed away with the effort she'd already expended, leaving her numb and oddly untethered, as though she had no reality, no anchor. If she did much more, she risked becoming a permanent ghostly resident of the Masterses household. If she returned to her solid form, she risked being controlled and used against Grey.

Nothing could've stopped her. Without a word to Essie, Rowan closed her eyes and pictured herself in the woods near where the girls always went in their trance.

When she opened her eyes, she found herself surrounded by pine trees and granite boulders, facing a battle of one against many.

She froze at the vision of Grey doing what he'd so clearly been born to do as he fought the wolves. Even through her terror for his life, Rowan was still mesmerized by the powerful display.

Three wolves already lay on the ground, one body still aflame. A sandy-colored wolf ran at Grey full tilt. His face a study of fierce concentration, Grey whispered a single word, and another bolt of blue lightning shot from his hands. The creature howled in pain before the lightning disappeared and it collapsed to the ground, tendrils of smoke rising from its body.

Rowan didn't have time to watch more as she caught sight of the black wolf. Kaios's lover had snuck around behind Grey, using the trees and her coloring as cover, but Rowan could see the green glow of her eyes in the radiance Grey's lightning had briefly cast in the small clearing.

Grey, busy with another two wolves, one of which went flying through the trees at his whispered word, didn't see the she-wolf behind him. Rowan couldn't yell out to warn him, or the wolf he faced would attack. But she didn't have enough magic left to stop the black wolf.

At that moment a tiny hummingbird came darting out of the trees. It hovered in front of Rowan. *"We're here."*

Before she could ask, animals of all kinds—elk, deer, mountain lions, even chipmunks and birds—stampeded into the clearing, going after all the wolves.

"What the—" Grey lowered his hands. But his back was still turned to the black wolf.

The bitch gathered herself, muscles bunching, to leap.

With an otherworldly sound that sent fear cascading down Rowan's spine, even in the spirit realm, she lunged.

But Grey spun to face her and knocked her back with a blast of energy. Blue lightning in an orb that should've fried her ass.

Only she stayed on her feet, lips curled over her teeth, eyes glowing, and lunged again.

Again he knocked her back.

But she just kept coming.

And with each spell cast, Grey wasn't just losing ground, he was using up his energy.

"Fuck," he muttered, his expression a cast of concentration.

Another lunge, only this time, he tried something else. Making a spinning move with his finger and with a whisper of words, a miniature tornado of wind whipped the wolf up, casting her about wildly.

Manifesting nature was almost as exhausting as forming energy from nothing. He wasn't going to be able to hold much longer.

But apparently Grey realized that. Because, suddenly, he stopped the twister, dirt and debris froze, and so did the wolf, about thirty feet up in the air. Then everything dropped to the ground. Only she managed to hop off one branch then another on her way down. Landing before Grey unharmed.

"Help him," Rowan urged any animals in the area, hoping like all the hells they could hear her.

With a snarl, she hurtled through the air, deadly jaw wide open.

Grey's hands shot up and froze her in place. Only immediately, he grimaced as though she'd struck him just the same. Holding an ancient werewolf had to be draining what little he had left inside him.

A terrifying roar erupted from the forest, and the massive grizzly bear who'd once warned Rowan of danger burst out into the clearing. He slammed into the black wolf mid-air. Coming down on top of her, he clamped his massive jaws around her head. With a twist and a sickening crunch, he snapped her neck.

Grey dropped to his knees, chest heaving from the effort.

Those wolves still alive, seeing their leader's lifeless form and the forces gathered against them, took off through the woods, Rowan's defenders in pursuit.

Rowan let out a whoop of relief. "Grey," she turned toward him, then sucked in a breath.

Three streaks of red crossed the white of his shirt, growing larger with every passing moment as blood spilled out of him. Apparently, the she-wolf had struck her mark before the bear had intercepted her. With a cough that brought blood bubbling up out of his mouth, Grey dropped to his knees before falling over to lie on his back, legs jacked up awkwardly beneath him.

"No," the word tore out of her.

In a blink Rowan was at his side. She closed her eyes, reaching for her body, willing herself back into the realm of the living, but nothing happened. She didn't have enough energy left to get herself out of the ghostly realm.

Grey was dying before her eyes, and she could do nothing but watch as she herself let go of life. Another gurgle of blood spilled out of his mouth as he choked on the liquid filling his lungs, and a new determination surged through her. She was lost, but maybe she had enough left in her to save him. Acting on pure instinct, Rowan held her hands over his chest and pulled from the magic deep inside her the energy produced by her very soul.

A whispered word, and her hands, even in this muted realm between life and death, began to glow—softly at first, then brighter until the light was almost blinding. Then, just as slowly, the light faded away. Under her hands, Grey's chest no longer bore the marks of death. Blood no longer pooled under his body.

"Rowan?" His deep voice brought her gaze to his face. Miraculously, he seemed to be looking directly at her. "How is this possible?" he asked. He shook his head, eyes dazed. "What are you?"

Rowan gave him a sad smile. "I'm—"

Cold in the form of biting pain slid through her bones

and took over every inch of her. With a gasp, Rowan held up her hands only to find the shadowy image of her fingers disappearing. Gods, she was vanishing so fast.

"What's going on?" Panic laced Grey's voice.

She didn't have time.

They didn't have time.

"Greyson Masters..." Her voice echoed through the trees around them. She reached for him, but most of her was gone. "I love you."

Chapter Twenty-Two

"No!" The word burst from inside him.

The woman he loved. The woman he'd claimed with his heart, his body, and his soul—had faded from all existence before his very eyes.

He'd fallen to the ground, knowing the injuries he sustained from that damn wolf were fatal. But warmth had lit inside his chest, and he'd opened his eyes to discover a bright glow hovering above him, and the breathtaking image of Rowan's face in the darkness beyond, her hair flowing around her more black than red.

And now she was gone.

He jumped to his feet and sprinted for the house. Grey had no fucking clue what was going on, but no way in hell was he losing Rowan. Not now. Not when he'd finally found her. The burning sigil on his chest told him this story couldn't be over yet.

Grey burst into the house intending to bring every mage, every creature with power, here to fix this. He had to save her.

He pulled up short at the sight of his daughters, standing

in a circle in the middle of the family room among shards of glass from the shattered windows, and most of the furniture toppled over. Hands clasped, they swayed and glowed, like they did in the forest.

"Is Rowan still here?" Chloe asked.

She kept her eyes trained on the center of the circle, appearing to listen. So did Lachlyn and Atleigh.

"Girls?" he asked. Not expecting an answer.

"Grandma Essie's here, Dad," Atleigh answered, even as she kept her gaze locked on whatever she saw. Shock retreated behind a tidal wave of emotions he had no hope of sorting out.

"Is Rowan there, too?"

Atleigh gave a small shake of her head. But she stopped mid-shake, her shoulders stiffening. "Is that possible?"

Grey's heart thundered inside him. Was what possible?

The three took a shuddering breath all at the same time.

He couldn't handle the stress. "What?" he urged. "Is what possible?"

"Grandma Essie says Rowan isn't completely gone. Not yet."

"Please save her," Lachlyn's cry burst from her and about broke his heart.

"Save her, Grandma," Chloe cried out next, Atleigh echoing her.

"Save her. Save Rowan." His daughters' voices entwined and wound together. Repeating the words, the pleas. In the glow of their power, tears seeped from his daughters' eyes.

Then suddenly they stopped, silence crashing down around them, sucking the sound from the room.

"Thank you," Chloe whispered, the words breaking.

"Dad," Lachlyn said. "She can save her with your help." They still stared into the center of the circle where nothing stood.

"How?" Anything.

"Do exactly as we say. Okay?"

He nodded.

"Stand in the corner that's always cold." The command came from all three girls. Emotionless. Like a chant.

Grey rushed to do their bidding, shivering as a draft of chilly air brushed over his skin in the spot by the fireplace. "The cold you feel is Grandma Essie."

Had she been here all this time?

"Gather your magic inside you," the girls intoned. "Be ready."

Grey closed his eyes, drawing on every reserve inside him, allowing the magic to tingle through his blood, pooling into his chest and creating warmth on the edge of burning.

"Repeat these words... *Satu Arammu Ina Etu Mitu Adi Nuru*."

He could be repeating the recipe to end every life in the world for all he understood. The words must be ancient. As soon as he spoke them, the warmth of the energy inside him drained, leaving a cold, dark void in its wake.

But, somehow, he wasn't tired. At first, nothing happened. Then a pinpoint of light came to life beside him. As he watched, an old woman materialized before his eyes. "Grandma Essie?"

She nodded. "I've been watching over you since the day I died," she said. Her voice sounded like Rowan's had earlier, as though she were speaking down a tunnel or on one of those old phonographs. "Though I didn't know I'd do this."

"Do what?"

"I am giving up my essence, my soul, to bring your Rowan back from the brink."

Everything inside him locked up. "What does that mean?"

Already, her aged figure was fading, as Rowan's had in the woods. "It's all right. I'm going to be with your grandfather now."

The moment too much to process, he could only nod. He stared at the face of a woman he'd known such a short time in life, but whose love he could feel radiating throughout the room. He stared as she faded to nothing, till only a shadow of her eyes lingered. And then…she was gone.

But where was Rowan?

He glanced at his girls, who stood in their trance, unmoving. They waited in silence for what felt like an interminable age. Then Chloe gasped.

He couldn't see anything.

"We can see her," they said in unison.

"Where?"

"Here." A few long moments passed before the girls spoke again. "Rowan? Can you hear us?"

A pause and he held his breath.

"Can you get back to us?" they asked next.

He couldn't see her or any reaction from his children. Just nothing. "What's happening?"

"Watch." Atleigh nodded to the spot toward which she was talking.

As he watched, suddenly the blurry vision of a woman started to materialize. At first so faint he couldn't see her features, the lines and edges of her face and body came into sharper and sharper focus. "Rowan," he whispered.

He started forward, but the girls held their circle closed against him. "Wait."

It took every ounce of willpower not to rush across the space to Rowan's side, but he did as he was told. Sure enough, her figure started to solidify before his eyes. The process was agonizing to watch. If Rowan's ragged breathing and pained expression were anything to go by, the process didn't appear pleasant to experience, either.

Finally, with a gut-wrenching moan, Rowan fell to her hands and knees, whole and with him, heaving with the effort.

At the same time, the girls let go of one another, the glow disappearing as they blinked owlishly, almost seeming lost. He had no idea who to run to first.

"We're okay, Dad," Lachlyn said.

"Rowan needs you," Atleigh added.

He didn't even remember crossing the room. He just knew he was at Rowan's side, pulling her shaking body into his arms. "You came back to us."

She took a shuddering breath, her entire body quivering. "Your grandmother…"

Her voice was hardly a whisper, and he smoothed her hair back from her face. "Shhhh… Rest now. My grandmother helped you, but she's passed on. She's with my grandfather now, she said."

She sagged, her eyes fluttering closed, the lashes starkly dark against her too-pale skin. "You shouldn't love me," she mumbled just before her head lolled back, out cold.

Chapter Twenty-Three

Soft sunlight filtered through Rowan's closed eyes, but she had no desire to wake up and face the world. Not yet.

"Sorry. But you must get up. Now."

Rowan frowned at the female voice annoyingly trying to pull her out of her slumber. She knew that voice. "Delilah?"

"I'm here. And I've let you sleep as long as I could. You need to get up and shower and dress. We have a meeting to attend."

A meeting? What in the eye of newt was the woman going on about?

"With the Covens Syndicate." Right then, the sound of a feline growl had Delilah swearing. "And get this damn cat away from me."

Memories came flooding back, along with a slam of fear, and a lance of pain spiked through Rowan's head. Oh, my... The wolf shifters. Grey. She'd...died.

Adrenaline spiking through her veins, Rowan peeled her eyes open to find Delilah sitting beside her bed in her room in Grey's basement, appearing her usual elegant self in a cream-colored cashmere sweater over black slacks, her dark hair coiled at her nape, loose tendrils framing her face. "What happened?"

Delilah hitched her lips in a half smile. "Grey's girls are ghost whisperers. They got someone named Essie to pull you out of there."

Essie? Grey's grandmother's ghost? How was that possible?

"No time to explain now, I have to get you to this meeting. Your fight's not over, Rowan. Time to confess all to your people."

The cold claws of fear reached in and rendered her numb and terrified at the same time. Grey was going to hate her, and she was about to be imprisoned or killed.

"I won't let them hurt you," Delilah said.

And that was the only reason Rowan allowed the other woman to tug her out of bed. In a whirlwind of movement, she was handed clothes and shoved into the bathroom.

"Wait."

Delilah paused in the act of closing the door and raised her eyebrows.

"Where's Grey?"

Delilah's lips thinned, her expression grim. "Already there."

• • •

Rowan clenched her hands against the shaking, which wouldn't stop. She wasn't entirely sure if the tremors were part of recovering from being mostly dead for a while or confronting the truth of who she was in front of the Covens Syndicate, particularly without having had a chance to talk to Grey in private first.

Couldn't be helped now.

She'd teleported them to the location Delilah provided

and now walked the halls of the ultramodern building where the Syndicate apparently held their meetings. She'd gone from mountain cabin to alien spaceship, though in the Sierra Nevadas now. Maybe she was still a ghost, and this was all a weird vision?

Delilah stopped at a mahogany door and rapped her knuckles sharply against it. Before Rowan could collect herself, a deep male voice called to come in, and Delilah dragged her inside.

A group of witches and warlocks of various ages, their faces all cast in blank judgment, sat at a long metal and glass table facing the doorway. Behind them a wall of windows showed the mountains in all their splendor. But she couldn't appreciate the view over the treetops when her life hung in the balance. She sought and found Grey, seated off to her left beside a man with black hair and eerily piercing blue eyes so pale they appeared almost white, reminding her of dragon shifters from the White Clan. Glacial. Her heart shriveled at the hard stare Grey directed her way.

Okay. This wasn't going to go well, then. She tried not to let the crack splitting her heart break it wide open. Not here in front of everyone.

"Ms. McAuliffe?" the man beside Grey asked, his deep tones almost bored.

Rowan nodded. His unusual gaze shifted to the woman at her side. "And you must be Ms.?"

Rowan glanced over to see Delilah give him a cool smile. "Delilah."

"First or last?"

Delilah said nothing, merely held her polite smile and the man's stare. There was someone in a position of power who didn't know her? If Rowan wasn't terrified, she'd have been more interested in that byplay.

After a long, intense moment, he let it go, turning back

to Rowan. "I'm Alasdair Blakesley, current head of the Syndicate. Greyson has filled us in on the situation and"—he flicked a glance at Delilah—"supplied us information provided by various witnesses."

Okay. She chanced a glance at Grey, who regarded her with zero expression. What had he told them?

"Now we'd like to hear from you."

Right.

She took a big breath, ignoring the way her hands shook uncontrollably, and tipped up her chin. "My name is Rowan McAuliffe. As a child I took on the last name of Tanya McAuliffe, the woman who raised me after my parents died. My birth parents were Cormac and Evelyn Balfour."

A ripple of movement shifted through the group before her. No surprise there. Balfour was one of the oldest names among their people.

"That's not possible. Your file lists a low-level magical couple named the Campbells."

Rowan turned her attention to Persephone. What was she doing here anyway? She sat there, in a deep red dress, her hair coiled in an elegant chignon, with an expression of suppressed glee.

"Then your files are wrong." Rowan glanced at Delilah, who smiled serenely, not fooling Rowan. The woman had somehow managed to alter the files.

"Cormac and Evelyn Balfour…and their daughter…were killed in a car crash," Persephone insisted.

Rowan shrugged a shoulder. "The woman who raised me found the wreck. She used a unique brand of magic to fake my death and took me away, passing me off as her own."

Alasdair flicked his finger over a tablet. Looking at paperwork? "This is Tanya McAuliffe? A common witch with limited powers?"

Rowan's mouth kicked up in a smile, despite the way

cold fear spread though her. No going back after this. "Tanya McAuliffe, a demon posing as a witch."

Even Delilah sucked in a breath, though Rowan doubted the Syndicate members caught the sound. Rowan, meanwhile, tried not to take a step back, anticipating the spell that would end her life.

But none came.

Her gaze flashed to Grey's to find him watching her closely. Surely, he would warn her if death were imminent? Even if he hated her right now.

Into the void of silence, Rowan continued hesitantly. "Tanya believed the crash that killed my parents wasn't an accident. She claimed someone was after me and thought maybe someone in the Syndicate. She hid me in plain sight as a"—she glanced at Persephone, chin going up—"common witch with limited powers. In secret, she taught me magic. A different kind from what you know. More powerful, using ancient words to power the spells."

"Impossible," an older gentleman hissed from the other end of the table.

Rowan ignored him. "It's only since living with...Mr. Masters that I've started to question Tanya's assumption. My guess now is that Kaios, the ancient werewolf who took me, was the one after me all along."

It made sense, once she'd been able to see past that lifelong fear of the people in this room. Tanya's fear. Grey had shown her that. With who he was and what he stood for. Even killing that warlock had been an act of honor. For his wife.

She tried to let him see that now, in her eyes. Only he looked away.

Still, she had to believe in him. He wouldn't let her die here today.

"Where is this Tanya now?" Alasdair asked.

"Dead." She took a deep breath, closing her eyes. She

could still hear Tanya's screams as that warlock kept her locked down and Kaios ripped her to shreds, followed by a silence which hurt even worse.

"Why would a werewolf want you?" Persephone sneered.

"Because I'm an Aneval."

Grey jerked his head to the side, looking away from her, and she knew he was remembering the animals in the forest that had saved their lives.

"And why would they care about that?" Persephone demanded. No doubt the poor woman wasn't too happy to discover Grey's powerless little nanny was actually something rather special.

"All animals have a certain draw for me. Shifters, to a certain extent, can dictate what I do. But, werewolves, because of their own brand of magic and the way it's tied to their animal form, can...call to me. The more powerful, ancient ones—" She shook her head and had to consciously force her jaw to unclench. "They can control me or any other Aneval. It's how Kaios got me to work against the demigod and witch I attacked, but my powers didn't work against the wolf shifters. I think to his surprise."

"Why did you not come to us in the first place? When Kaios was killed and you were released from his control?" Alasdair asked.

She grimaced. "I'd been raised to question if the Syndicate killed my parents. Then you killed the other warlock Kaios used without any understanding of why he did what he did, or that's how it appeared at the time."

Alasdair glanced at Grey, whose face seemed to have turned to granite, then sat forward. "Are you saying we killed an innocent man?"

"I know better now," she said softly. "I learned the truth, and it made me start to question my beliefs. But the kind of trust you're asking for takes...a lot."

Again, he slid his gaze to Grey, who didn't move.

Alasdair turned back to her. "Does that alleviate your concern about us?"

She blinked, pulling her focus back to the leader of all mages. "It...helps." Given her upbringing, full trust would take time. "I'd rather not be locked up or killed because werewolves can control me."

Persephone jumped to her feet. "Of *course* you should be execu—"

"Don't you fucking say it," Grey snapped the words so loud they seemed to bounce off the windows.

Persephone whipped a glare his direction. "But her kind are dangerous."

He still wasn't looking at Rowan. "No more than you or I. Sit down."

After her mouth opening and closing a few times, Persephone did as he said. Then Grey nodded at Alasdair.

And Rowan had no idea what to do with any of that. Was he defending her? Did he hate her, but not enough to kill her? *Look at me,* she urged.

Alasdair, meanwhile, regarded her with a long, intent look before relaxing back in his seat. "So...why the deception, posing as Greyson's nanny?"

Delilah put a hand on Rowan's arm. "I'm afraid that was my idea. Rowan didn't trust you, but I knew she needed the protection only her own people could offer. I know Greyson. I trust him. I sent her with the idea that she would hide in plain sight and try to thwart his investigation, but my hope was that they would earn each other's trust. A Seer confirmed this to be the best course of action. Unfortunately, Kaios's lover forced our hand."

The trust thing was all news to Rowan. "I should've known you had a bigger plan," she muttered under her breath.

Delilah squeezed her arm before releasing her, her only

acknowledgment.

"I see," Alasdair said. "Just so we're clear…you descend from one of our most ancient families. You're an Aneval, and werewolves can control you. You were raised by a demon. Anything else?"

Persephone's expression reminded Rowan of an old woman in her village in Ireland whose face had drawn in on itself, giving her the constant expression of having sucked on a lemon. But Rowan could find no joy in the moment, because Persephone wasn't important. Grey was, and he wouldn't look at her anymore. Like he couldn't stand the sight of her.

Rowan considered telling them about the sigil on her wrist, but that was between her and Grey. And, should the Syndicate decide to execute her, she didn't want him to know. She couldn't bear it if she hurt him that way. "No." Was it possible to die from a shattered heart? "Nothing else."

Alasdair swiveled to Grey. "Anything to add?"

Rowan locked eyes with the man she loved, trying to plead with him, to communicate the truth—that she'd never hurt him or the girls. *I'm sorry,* she mouthed.

He glanced away, moving his gaze to Alasdair. "You have all the information you need."

Rowan looked down and bit the inside of her cheek to keep the tears at bay. She wouldn't forgive her, either, if she were in his position. But she'd hoped.

Silly, really. To believe he could.

Alasdair turned back to them. "Wait in one of our smaller conference rooms. Michael, who's waiting outside the door, will show you where. One of us will meet you there with our decision."

Grey still wouldn't look at her. Persephone's sour lemon expression turned into the smirk of a cat who'd guzzled a gallon of cream, and Rowan's feet refused to move. Delilah had to tug at her arm, practically pulling her out of the room.

Chapter Twenty-Four

Grey blew out a long breath before he turned the knob and entered the room where Rowan waited with Delilah. The Syndicate, with a big push from Alasdair, had sided with his recommendations. It helped that Rowan had used her powers to protect him and his family and help kill Kaios's people. Now he had to see if Rowan would go along with what they were going to ask of her.

Everything—his entire life—depended on her response.

She'd said she loved him. He'd heard her through the haze of death she'd yanked him out of the night the wolves attacked. Had she meant it?

Sitting through Rowan's interrogation had been one of the most difficult things he'd ever done. His own personal hell—to sit and do nothing. To not defend her at the top of his lungs. To not show her in any way that he wouldn't let them hurt her. Snarling at Persephone had been a slip. Unavoidable. No one was killing or locking Rowan away. Not while he had breath in his body.

Of anyone in that room, he'd been most at risk from her,

and he should be the most pissed at her. He should've been furious at her deceptions, incensed that, after what they'd shared, she still hadn't trusted him with the truth. But, after she'd risked her own life to protect the girls and save him...his only thought had been protecting her from the very people he served. From his own job.

He'd spent the last three days doing so.

Grey walked into the small conference room to find Rowan standing at the window staring out at the view of the mountains. Delilah sat in a chair calmly tapping away on her cell phone, her long nails clicking against the screen. Both women turned when he entered.

"I'll leave you two alone," Delilah murmured.

He gave her a nod of thanks but barely noticed as she left, closing the door behind her with a soft *click*, leaving total silence in her wake.

Rowan eyed him warily, her arms crossed over her stomach like she was holding herself together. "So...what did they decide?"

Grey stepped closer. "Do you remember the night you told the girls a story about a pony who went to live with a family of donkeys, hoping to hide from the master who wanted to send her to the glue factory?"

She blinked at him, then frowned. "You know about those stories?"

Grey watched her, searching for any sign of her true feelings. This witch had sent his emotions into a tailspin. He had no idea what had been real between them and what had been an act to survive. "I listened outside the door almost every night."

"Oh." She glanced away.

"Was that story about you?"

That pulled her gaze back to him, and he could see the questions and doubts swirling there. She opened her mouth to answer, then took a deep breath. "Yes."

"In the story, the pony ends up wishing she could stay with the donkeys forever," he murmured.

Again she opened her mouth and closed it. "What did they decide, Grey?"

He blew out a sharp breath, no closer to the answers he needed and with no clue how she'd respond to what he was about to say. "That depends on you."

She frowned. "Me?"

"Yes. You won't be punished if you agree to certain conditions."

Rowan's already pale skin blanched, those adorable freckles across the bridge of her nose standing out in stark relief. He took another step closer but held back from going to her. They needed to work this out first.

"They want you to teach them the magic you were taught by the demon."

She glanced down at her hands and appeared to consider that, then nodded, her gaze back to his. "All right."

"You work with other Anevals to both spread the word about this vulnerability their power creates, and also to work with werewolves we trust to develop magic to protect you and the others."

Now interest sparked in her eyes, the wariness easing. "Which werewolves?"

"That will be determined later, but I'll make sure they're safe."

Again, she nodded. "Done."

Her instant trust eased something inside him.

"What else?" she asked.

"You stay with me for the foreseeable future."

Now she frowned. Not the reaction he was hoping for. "As your...prisoner?"

He hid a wince that she could even think that. Grey

stepped closer, right into her personal space, inhaling the wildflower and honey scent of her, wanting to hold her, but they weren't there yet. Rowan didn't back away, but she still regarded him with wary, wide eyes, swirling with darker gray, like a storm. "Not as my prisoner."

"As what then?"

"I want to give you a set place in this life."

The flutter of her pulse at the base of her throat kicked up a notch, and the hope gleaming in her silver eyes couldn't be just a trick of the light. Gods, he'd better not be seeing things he wished to see.

"What do you mean?" she asked.

"As a bonded pair. You and me."

He caught her soft gasp, her eyes dilating. "You know about that?"

Shock spiraled through him, clenching the muscles in his arms, pulling his hands into fists. What was she talking about? He hadn't officially bonded with her yet, and they hadn't talked about love. "What do you mean? You already knew?"

Rowan's brows drew down. "I…" She bit her lip. "Do you *want* to bond with me?"

Grey couldn't stand the uncertainty in her eyes a second longer. He reached out and ran a finger along her smooth cheek. "I fell in love with you the day you walked into my house and froze the girls mid-fight and all I could think about was kissing these freckles and that I wasn't all on my own anymore." He lightly touched the end of her nose. "You brought laughter back into my life, and into the girls' lives. You filled a gaping hole inside me I didn't realize was eating at me until you showed up."

Big gray eyes gazed up at him, still uncertain.

"Let me show you something." Grey undid the top few buttons of his shirt and pulled the material aside to show her his family sigil tattooed on his chest. He took her by the wrist and guided her fingers to the mark. As soon as she touched it, the tattoo glowed red, like a brand held to the fire.

Rowan gasped. Then the most beautiful smile he'd ever seen stole across her face, lighting her up from the inside. "Let me show you something, too." She pulled her hand out of his loose grasp and flipped her arm over, pulling back the sleeve of her sweater.

There, glowing white, was a smaller version of his sigil. The breath punched out of his lungs, even as his body responded to the sight of his mark on Rowan's skin. Bonded pairs among witches happened only when soul-deep love was involved. A magical connection that their kind didn't enter into lightly because it could alter their magic. Even with Maddie he hadn't considered entering into a bonding. But with Rowan... Still, it was supposed to be a choice. A spell. "When? How?"

Rowan laughed, the husky sound kicking through him. "The day we met. It took a while to fully form, so I didn't know."

Fascinated, Grey lightly ran a finger over her mark, enjoying the hiss of air his touch elicited from her. He smiled but released her. If hers felt anything like his at physical touch from her bonded other half, then if he didn't stop, they'd be naked and on the floor in short order. He'd rather save that for when they got home.

First, he needed to know. He took her face in his hands and gazed into those gorgeous gray eyes that no longer stared at him with wary question but glowed with...hope. "Will you be my bonded other half, Rowan?"

She smiled softly. "I think it's too late to stop."

He didn't return the smile, needing an answer.

Without his saying more, she seemed to understand. "Somewhere between trying to protect myself from you and then trying to help you with the girls, I fell in love with you, Greyson Masters. With all of you. Spending the rest of my life at your side won't be long enough. I don't need any sigil to tell me something my heart already knows."

Unable to resist any longer, he laid his lips over hers, claiming her in the most basic way, with a kiss. He savored and sipped at her for a long while before pulling back, allowing his gaze to take in every curve and angle of her face. "I love you, too."

She dimpled, eyes sparkling at him. Then she sobered. "The girls?"

"Helped save you because they love you. They will be thrilled. They love you as much as I do."

Again, that glowing smile stole his breath. "That is a relief."

He stole a kiss in return. "Let's go home."

She gave a contented sigh. "All I ever wanted, and never thought I could have, was to call your home my home."

He put his forehead to hers, closing his eyes and inhaling, letting the tension go with the knowledge that she'd be his forever. "For the rest of our lives. I can hardly believe this is real. Maybe I died in that spirit realm."

He took her hand and put it over his beating heart so she could feel for herself his heat and the thumping tumble of beats inside his chest. "It's real. All of it."

Epilogue

Delilah walked away from the door with zero remorse at listening in but satisfied the situation had finally been resolved to her liking. Rowan and Greyson had not been a foregone conclusion. Nor had been the Covens Syndicate decision not to imprison or kill Rowan, given her background and actions.

Now Delilah could turn her full attention to other clients whom she'd basically put on a back burner for the last few weeks as this situation had needed her full attention. She had to check in with Nico on his investigation of the woman who kept fading from sight. And a request to find a supernatural doctor to send up north to attend to an isolated town of elves had recently hit her desk. Except paranormal doctors were a rare breed.

Lost in her thoughts, only finely tuned instinct saved her from being knocked on her ass when a door opened right in her path, stopping inches from her face.

The door closed to reveal the imposing form of Alasdair Blakesley. She kept her expression bland, despite her pounding heart, which had nothing to do with almost being clobbered by the door and everything to do with the visceral reaction this man pulled from her with merely a glance.

How had she not come across this warlock before?

"Excuse me," she murmured, and went to walk around him.

"Delilah."

She turned, refusing to acknowledge what his deep voice did to her. "Yes?"

"Your manipulations worked out."

She raised her eyebrows coolly and said nothing.

"That is the only reason I'm allowing you to walk out of here unchallenged and unscathed."

Irritation spiked through her blood, along with a reaction she hadn't felt in years: challenge. "I'll keep that in mind."

She turned to go, only to be stopped by his hand on her arm, his touch insistent and dragging an immediate reaction of need from her reluctant body.

"I don't make this warning lightly," he murmured.

"I believe you."

"Stay away from my people."

Now she cocked her head. "I'll stay away from them if they stay away from me and my clients."

Alasdair's lips thinned, his eyes like ice chips. "I understand you have quite a varied clientele. That could prove…difficult."

She shrugged. His problem. Not hers.

He considered her for a long moment, and she refused to look away from his stare. After a moment, his lips hitched in a shadow of a smile. "Will you at least contact me if witches are involved?"

Delilah pursed her lips. She disliked being cornered or beholden to anyone. "I can't make guarantees, because it may depend on my client and the privacy privileges they hold with me. But I will when I can. That's the best I can do."

He inclined his head, though his jaw hardened. "Fair enough."

She glanced down at his hand still on her arm, studying his long, tapered fingers and a burn mark across the side. Interesting. "May I go?"

Now he did smile, a real one that reached his eyes, and she sucked in a sharp breath. "I'll see you again, I'm sure."

Delilah turned on her stiletto heels and clacked down the hallway, uncomfortably aware of his gaze on her until she rounded a bend.

Not if I see you first.

Acknowledgments

I get to do what I love surrounded by the people I love—a blessing that I thank God for every single day. Writing and publishing a book doesn't happen without the support and help from a host of incredible people.

To my fantastic, paranormal romance readers… Thanks for going on these journeys with me, for your kindness, your support, and generally being awesome. Rowan and Grey's romance was one that took more twists than even I expected. I hope you fell in love with these characters and their story as much as I did. If you have a free sec, please think about leaving a review. Also, I love to connect with my readers, so I hope you'll drop a line and say "Howdy" on any of my social media!

To my editor, Heather Howland…as always, working with you is the best time I have with writing my stories.

To my Entangled team…best in the business and awesome friends.

To my agent, Evan Marshall… Thank you for your constant support.

To my support team of friends, sprinting partners, beta readers, critique partners, writing buddies, reviewers, and family (you know who you are)... I know I say this every time, but I mean it... My stories wouldn't come alive the way they do if I didn't have the wonderful experiences and support that I do. And that's all because of you.

Finally, to my own bonded partner...I love you so much. To our awesome kids, I don't know how it's possible, but I love you more every day. I can't wait to see the story of your own lives.

About the Author

Award-winning paranormal romance author Abigail Owen grew up consuming books and exploring the world through her writing. She loves to write witty, feisty heroines, sexy heroes who deserve them, and a cast of lovable characters to surround them (and maybe get their own stories). She currently resides in Austin, Texas, with her own personal hero, her husband, and their two children, who are growing up way too fast.

Fury Unleashed
a *Forgotten Brotherhood* novel by N.J. Walters

Maccus Fury, a fallen angel, is trying hard to keep his sanity. Seems being an assassin might be catching up with him. Now, Heaven, or Hell, has sent a beautiful assassin to kill him. Lovely. She's smart and snarky––but she has no idea what she's walked into. And he's more than peeved that they only sent one person. They're going to need an army if they want him dead.

Pirate's Persuasion
a *Sentinels of Savannah* novel by Lisa Kessler

Immortal pirate Drake Cole has a painful secret—when the Sea Dog sank in 1795, a young stowaway, whom Drake swore a blood oath to protect, went down with the ship. The ghost of a boy lost at sea over two hundred years ago leads local medium Heather Storrey right to Drake's door. She's determined to free him from his self-imposed prison. But how can she protect him from a curse no one can see?

MALFUNCTION
a *Dark Desires Origin* novel by Nina Croft

It's been five hundred years since we fled a dying Earth. Twenty-four ships, each carrying ten thousand humans—Chosen Ones—sleeping peacefully...until people start dying in cryo. Malfunction or murder? Sergeant Logan Farrell is determined to find the truth. Katia Mendoza, hot-shot homicide detective, has been woken from cryo to assist his investigation, and Logan finds himself falling for her. But he doesn't know Katia's secret... It's not only humans who fled the dying Earth.

NIGHT'S KISS
an *Ancients* novel by Mary Hughes

Vampires killed my parents before my eyes when I was young. My revenge? I'll destroy every last one of the evil bastards, starting with their king. But only one man can help me find him. Achingly tall, dark, and too-sexy-for-his-own-good, Ryker. Now it seems evil monsters are also after our prey, and they'll stop at nothing to see us all dead. And why are we having so much trouble finding the king?

Made in United States
Troutdale, OR
06/17/2024

20622422R00135